THE GINGER JAR
CAPER

Volume 5: Zen and the Art of Investigation

ANTHONY WOLFF

authorHOUSE®

AuthorHouse™
1663 Liberty Drive
Bloomington, IN 47403
www.authorhouse.com
Phone: 1-800-839-8640

This is a work of fiction. All of the characters, names, incidents, organizations, and dialogue in this novel are either the products of the author's imagination or are used fictitiously.

Published by AuthorHouse 03/05/2014

ISBN: 978-1-4918-6659-7 (sc)
ISBN: 978-1-4918-6657-3 (e)

PREFACE

WHO ARE THESE DETECTIVES ANYWAY?

"The eye cannot see itself" an old Zen adage informs us. The Private I's in these case files count on the truth of that statement. People may be self-concerned, but they are rarely self-aware.

In courts of law, guilt or innocence often depends upon its presentation. Juries do not - indeed, they may not - investigate any evidence in order to test its veracity. No, they are obliged to evaluate only what they are shown. Private Investigators, on the other hand, are obliged to look beneath surfaces and to prove to their satisfaction - not the court's - whether or not what appears to be true is actually true. The Private I must have a penetrating eye.

Intuition is a spiritual gift and this, no doubt, is why *Wagner & Tilson, Private Investigators* does its work so well.

At first glance the little group of P.I.s who solve these often baffling cases seem different from what we (having become familiar with video Dicks) consider "sleuths." They have no oddball sidekicks. They are not alcoholics. They get along well with cops.

George Wagner is the only one who was trained for the job. He obtained a degree in criminology from Temple University in Philadelphia and did exemplary work as an investigator with the Philadelphia Police. These were his golden years. He skied; he danced; he played tennis; he had a Porsche, a Labrador retriever, and a small sailboat. He got married and had a wife, two toddlers, and a house. He was handsome and well built, and he had great hair.

And then one night, in 1999, he and his partner walked into an ambush. His partner was killed and George was shot in the left knee and in his right shoulder's brachial plexus. The pain resulting from his injuries and the twenty-two surgeries he endured throughout the year that followed, left him addicted to a nearly constant morphine drip. By the time he was admitted to a rehab center in Southern California for treatment of his morphine addiction and for physical therapy, he had lost everything previously mentioned except his house, his handsome face, and his great hair.

His wife, tired of visiting a semi-conscious man, divorced him and married a man who had more than enough money to make child support payments unnecessary and, since he was the jealous type, undesirable. They moved far away, and despite the calls George placed and the money and gifts he sent, they soon tended to regard him as non-existent. His wife did have an orchid collection which she boarded with a plant nursery, paying for the plants' care until he was able to accept them. He gave his brother his car, his tennis racquets, his skis, and his sailboat.

At the age of thirty-four he was officially disabled, his right arm and hand had begun to wither slightly from limited use, a frequent result of a severe injury to that nerve center. His knee, too, was troublesome. He could not hold it in a bent position for an extended period of time; and when the weather was bad or he had been standing for too long, he limped a little.

George gave considerable thought to the "disease" of romantic love and decided that he had acquired an immunity to it. He would never again be vulnerable to its delirium. He did not realize that the gods of love regard such pronouncements as hubris of the worst kind and, as such, never allow it to go unpunished. George learned this lesson while working on the case, *The Monja Blanca*. A sweet girl, half his age and nearly half his weight, would fell him, as he put it, "as young David slew the big dumb Goliath." He understood that while he had no future with her, his future would be filled with her for as long as he had a mind that could think. She had been the victim of the most vicious swindlers he had ever encountered. They had successfully fled the country, but not the range of George's determination to apprehend them. These were master criminals, four of them, and he secretly vowed that he would make them fall, one by one. This was a serious quest. There was nothing quixotic about George Roberts Wagner.

While he was in the hospital receiving treatment for those fateful gunshot wounds, he met Beryl Tilson.

Beryl, a widow whose son Jack was then eleven years old, was working her way through college as a nurse's aid when she tended George. She had met him previously when he delivered a lecture on the curious differences between aggravated assault and attempted murder, a not uninteresting topic. During the year she tended him, they became friendly enough for him to communicate with her during the year he was in rehab. When he returned to Philadelphia, she picked him up at the airport, drove him home - to a house he had not been inside for two years - and helped him to get settled into a routine with the house and the botanical spoils of his divorce.

After receiving her degree in the Liberal Arts, Beryl tried to find a job with hours that would permit her to be home when her son came home from school each day. Her quest was daunting. Not only was a degree in Liberal Arts regarded as a 'negative' when considering an applicant's qualifications, (the choice of study having demonstrated a lack of foresight for eventual entry into the commercial job market) but by stipulating that she needed to be home no later than 3:30 p.m. each day, she further discouraged personnel managers from putting out their company's welcome mat. The supply of available jobs was somewhat limited.

Beryl, a Zen Buddhist and karate practitioner, was still doing part-time work when George proposed that they open a private investigation agency. Originally he had thought she would function as a "girl friday" office manager; but when he witnessed her abilities in the martial arts, which, at that time, far exceeded his, he agreed that she should function as a 50-50 partner in the agency, and he helped her through the licensing procedure. She quickly became an excellent marksman on the gun range. As a Christmas gift he gave her a Beretta to use alternately with her Colt semi-automatic.

The Zen temple she attended was located on Germantown Avenue in a two storey, store-front row of small businesses. Wagner & Tilson, Private Investigators needed a home. Beryl noticed that a building in the same row was advertised for sale. She told George who liked it, bought it, and let Beryl and her son move into the second floor as their residence. Problem solved.

While George considered himself a man's man, Beryl did not see herself as a woman's woman. She had no female friends her own age. None. Acquaintances, yes. She enjoyed warm relationships with a few older women. But Beryl, it surprised her to realize, was a man's woman. She liked men, their freedom to move, to create, to discover, and that inexplicable wildness that came with their physical presence and strength. All of her senses found them agreeable; but she had no desire to domesticate one. Going to sleep with one was nice. But waking up with one of them in her bed? No. No. No. Dawn had an alchemical effect on her sensibilities. "Colors seen by candlelight do not look the same by day," said Elizabeth Barrett Browning, to which Beryl replied, "Amen."

She would find no occasion to alter her orisons until, in the course of solving a missing person's case that involved sexual slavery in a South American rainforest, a case called *Skyspirit*, she met the Surinamese Southern District's chief criminal investigator. Dawn became conducive to romance. But, as we all know, the odds are always against the success of long distance love affairs. To be stuck in one continent and love a man who is stuck in another holds as much promise for high romance as falling in love with Dorian Gray. In her professional life, she was tough but fair. In matters of lethality, she preferred *dim mak* points to bullets, the latter being awfully messy.

Perhaps the most unusual of the three detectives is Sensei Percy Wong. The reader may find it useful to know a bit more about his background.

Sensei, Beryl's karate master, left his dojo to go to Taiwan to become a fully ordained Zen Buddhist priest in the Ummon or Yun Men lineage in which he was given the Dharma name Shi Yao Feng. After studying advanced martial arts in both Taiwan and China, he returned to the U.S. to teach karate again and to open a small Zen Buddhist temple - the temple that was down the street from the office *Wagner & Tilson* would eventually open.

Sensei was quickly considered a great martial arts' master not because, as he explains, "I am good at karate, but because I am better at advertising it." He was of Chinese descent and had been ordained in China, and since China's Chan Buddhism and Gung Fu stand in polite rivalry to Japan's Zen Buddhism and Karate, it was most peculiar to find a priest in China's Yun Men lineage who followed the Japanese Zen liturgy and the martial arts discipline of Karate.

It was only natural that Sensei Percy Wong's Japanese associates proclaimed that his preferences were based on merit, and in fairness to them, he did not care to disabuse them of this notion. In truth, it was Sensei's childhood rebellion against his tyrannical faux-Confucian father that caused him to gravitate to the Japanese forms. Though both of his parents had emigrated from China, his father decried western civilization even as he grew rich exploiting its freedoms and commercial opportunities. With draconian finesse he imposed upon his family the cultural values of the country from which he had fled for his life. He seriously believed that while the rest of the world's population might have come out of Africa, Chinese men came out of heaven. He did not know or care where Chinese women originated so long as they kept their proper place as slaves.

His mother, however, marveled at American diversity and refused to speak Chinese to her children, believing, as she did, in the old fashioned idea that it is wise to speak the language of the country in which one claims citizenship.

At every turn the dear lady outsmarted her obsessively sinophilic husband. Forced to serve rice at every meal along with other mysterious creatures obtained in Cantonese Chinatown, she purchased two Shar Peis that, being from Macau, were given free rein of the dining room. These dogs, despite their pre-Qin dynasty lineage, lacked a discerning palate and proved to be gluttons for bowls of fluffy white stuff. When her husband retreated to his rooms, she served omelettes and Cheerios, milk instead of tea, and at dinner, when he was not there at all, spaghetti instead of chow mein. The family home was crammed with gaudy enameled furniture and torturously carved teak; but on top of the lion-head-ball-claw-legged coffee table, she always placed a book which illustrated the elegant simplicity of such furniture designers as Marcel Breuer; Eileen Gray; Charles Eames; and American Shakers. Sensei adored her; and loved to hear her relate how, when his father ordered her to give their firstborn son a Chinese name; she secretly asked the clerk to record indelibly the name "Percy" which she mistakenly thought was a very American name. To Sensei, if she had named him Abraham Lincoln Wong, she could not have given him a more Yankee handle.

Preferring the cuisines of Italy and Mexico, Sensei avoided Chinese food and prided himself on not knowing a word of Chinese. He balanced this ignorance by an inability to understand Japanese and, because of its inaccessibility, he did not eat Japanese food.

The Man of Zen who practices Karate obviously is the adventurous type; and Sensei, staying true to type, enjoyed participating in Beryl's and George's investigations. It required little time for him to become a one-third partner of the team. He called himself, "the ampersand in *Wagner & Tilson.*"

Sensei Wong may have been better at advertising karate than at performing it, but this merely says that he was a superb huckster for the discipline. In college he had studied civil engineering; but he also was on the fencing team and he regularly practiced gymnastics. He had learned yoga and ancient forms of meditation from his mother. He attained Zen's vaunted transcendental states; which he could access 'on the mat.' It was not surprising that when he began to learn karate he was already half-accomplished. After he won a few minor championships he attracted the attention of several martial arts publications that found his "unprecedented" switchings newsworthy. They imparted to him a "great master" cachet, and perpetuated it to the delight of dojo owners and martial arts shopkeepers. He did win many championships and, through unpaid endorsements and political propaganda, inspired the sale of Japanese weapons, including nunchaku and shuriken which he did not actually use.

Although his Order was strongly given to celibacy, enough wiggle room remained for the priest who found it expedient to marry or dally. Yet, having reached his mid-forties unattached, he regarded it as 'unlikely' that he would ever be romantically welded to a female, and as 'impossible' that he would be bonded to a citizen and custom's agent of the People's Republic of China - whose Gung Fu abilities challenged him and who would strike terror in his heart especially when she wore Manolo Blahnik red spike heels. Such combat, he insisted, was patently unfair, but he prayed that Providence would not level the playing field. He met his femme fatale while working on *A Case of Virga*.

Later in their association Sensei would take under his spiritual wing a young Thai monk who had a degree in computer science and a flair for acting. Akara Chatree, to whom Sensei's master in Taiwan would give the name Shi Yao Xin, loved Shakespeare; but his father - who came from one of Thailand's many noble families - regarded his son's desire to become an actor as we would regard our son's desire to become a hit man. Akara's brothers were all businessmen and professionals; and as the old patriarch lay dying, he exacted a promise from his tall 'matinee-idol' son that he would never tread upon the flooring of a stage. The old man had asked for nothing else, and since he bequeathed a rather large sum of money to his young son, Akara had to content himself with critiquing the performances of actors who were less filially constrained than he. As far as romance is concerned, he had not thought too much about it until he worked on *A Case of Industrial Espionage*. That case took him to Bermuda, and what can a young hero do when he is captivated by a pretty girl who can recite Portia's lines with crystalline insight while lying beside him on a white beach near a blue ocean?

But his story will keep...

FRIDAY, SEPTEMBER 9, 2011

It is not always wise to assume that because a person is a member of a race or nationality he or she conforms to popular notions about such ethnic groupings. The danger in the assumption consists in the motivational force that is necessary for the individual who separates himself from long held stereotypical identifications. When former police commissioner Terrell Maitlin needed a private investigator who knew something about antique Chinese porcelain and therefore thought that Sensei Percy Wong was the perfect person to call, he touched that "separation impetus" and got an adverse reaction that he did not expect.

Sensei, who happened to be sitting at Beryl Tilson's desk when the call came in, answered it. Maitlin introduced himself and asked, "Are you the Chinese detective?"

"I was born in Philadelphia." Sensei looked at the phone, wondering if the question had been the first line of a joke.

"Good," Maitlin said, relieved. "Then we won't have a language barrier. I need an investigator who is familiar with Chinese culture... language... history."

"I doubt that I'm your man," Sensei said. "Not all Frenchmen eat french fries and not all secretariats win the Triple Crown."

Maitlin sighed and apologized. "I must sound stupid. I'm a bit overwhelmed here... in over my head. All right. Let me start again. Do you know anything about antique Chinese porcelain?"

Images of his childhood home rolled through Sensei's mind with cinematic clarity. "Familiar only in the sense that my father had a few Ming and Qing dynasty ginger jars that he treated like religious icons."

1

Sensei became defensive and mentally drew a line to let Maitlin know which side he was on. "My mother preferred Wedgewood... as do I."

"Are you familiar with the fake Chinese porcelains' market?"

"I've read about it and I'm sure it exists - as does fake 'ancient Greek' pottery. I can't name any specific criminal who was caught creating or selling the pieces. To me, it's ordinary crime. It doesn't become sacrilegious because it's ancient Chinese art. What I mean is, fraud is fraud."

Maitlin spoke with relief. "If you're available, you're hired. I needed to hear a rational attitude towards this kind of crime. There's so much emotional drivel associated with a piece of fake art that it's impossible to discuss the subject without creating controversy. Can I engage your services? I'm a former police commissioner here in Washington State. Terrell Maitlin. My wife and I live just north of Seattle, in Everton."

"Frankly, Commissioner, you'd be better off getting someone locally. We don't go on out-of-state jobs singly. So you'd be paying for two investigators to travel across country. I'm not a full time investigator. My plate is full as it is - I'm a Zen Buddhist priest and I teach Karate. So, between Zendo and Dojo I'm pretty busy. Anyone who's got a problem that requires knowledge in a specific subject - banking, art, computers, Chinese culture - is better off finding a local expert in that field."

"I don't care if I have to pay for five of you to come across country. And I don't care what your fee is. Stephen Cioran recommended the Wagner & Tilson P.I. agency. I'm hoping I can get you here by Monday. I need someone I can trust. Stephen definitely trusts you—"

Sensei interrupted him. "Let me get George Wagner on a conference call. You can describe your problem to both of us at the same time. Hold on..."

Sensei, still holding the receiver, stood in the partition's opening. "George," he whispered, "Stephen Cioran of Seattle told this man, former police commissioner Terrell Maitlin, to call us. I said I'd put the three of us on a conference call. He wants us to come to Seattle by this Monday." George picked up the phone.

Terrell Maitlin summarized the problem. "I think part of the trouble my dear wife and I are having is due to my being a police commissioner which is essentially an honorific post. I've never been a police officer and I'm not a lawyer. I'm just a retired businessman. I sold insurance. People assumed that I knew something about law enforcement. I didn't. At Commission meetings I stayed silent until budgetary matters came up."

"What's the problem you're having?" George asked.

"I'll start with our dog Max. He's a trained German shepherd drug-sniffing dog that had retired from service. The officer who worked with him had taken him home as a pet. But the fellow died suddenly of a heart attack, so I volunteered to take the old dog in. Everything was fine at home. My children are all married and living elsewhere.

"My wife is a collector of Chinese porcelain. She regards herself as an authority on the stuff and is certain she can tell a fake piece when she sees one.

"One day she comes home from the antique dealer's with a big Chinese ginger jar. She knows this dealer - he's a man she's done business with and knows him to be both honest and knowledgeable - and the dog alerts to the jar. The dog knew the smell of illegal drugs and this jar had the smell on it. He was so excited that he made a little growling noise and planted himself at my wife's feet with his tail wagging. That's how he was trained to respond when he smelled drugs. She looked inside the jar and, sure enough, there was a small amount of white powder in the bottom. It's still there. She won't remove it, she says, until she gets some answers. We had to put Max outside so that my wife could take the jar up to our bedroom.

"She went to the dealer and tried to learn the jar's history, so to speak. He bought it from the museum here... the Wai Neng Chinese Porcelain Museum. They got it from a reputable dealer who's got offices in Singapore and Bangkok. She tells the museum people about the dog's reaction, and next thing we know there's a controversy about the jar's authenticity. She says it is an authentic Imperial Qing jar; but some people at the museum figure that it must be a fake and that the person who created it was probably a low-life drug user and got his scent all over the piece.

"I tell my wife that as a retired police commissioner I cannot allow my name to be dragged into any drug-related case or to be stupidly tricked by an art forger. I tell her to forget about the jar. But she is a stubborn woman. She knows her porcelain and nobody is going to tell her she doesn't. And it goes on and on and on."

George and Sensei looked at each other and grinned. George laughed. "I've been married, Mr. Maitlin. I know what you mean."

Maitlin laughed, too. "A wife who considers herself an expert in a field is like a juggernaut coming at you - you can't do anything but move out of its way. I don't care what your fee is - I can pay it - but I want results. Why is my dog smelling drugs on an allegedly antique Chinese ginger jar?"

George Wagner liked the idea of taking a case on the West Coast. He missed his kids who were in his ex-wife's custody in Northern California. Maybe he could arrange to visit them when the case was over. But that was a separate matter. The dog's reaction to an antique jar needed more in the way of explanation. "Mr. Maitlin," he said, "your dog is a trained detector of drugs; so the answer to the question of why he smells drugs has got to be because there are or were drugs there to smell. If the controversy is about the authenticity of the vase, we're not the people who can establish that. But your problem sounds to me to be a whole lot more serious.

"Consider this. A local ceramic's museum buys a jar from a reputable dealer and sells it to another reputable dealer who sells it to a local client, the antique-savvy wife of a police commissioner. That's four tiers of experts who regarded this jar as genuine. Now, suddenly, when there is a suspicion that the jar contained illegal drugs, it becomes a fake? No. This is a deliberate shift in focus... from a greater crime to a lesser one.

"If she called the DEA on the matter, they'd probably brush her off particularly if they already were investigating the principals."

"She did call them. And they did just that... brushed her off as though she were a lunatic of some kind."

"But, Mr. Maitlin, the fact remains that this is a matter for drug enforcement agents. This is not a case about art. It's about drug smuggling. What's most significant is that the museum people must somehow be involved. If they weren't, they would want to cooperate in discovering whether someone at the source of the shipment needs to be investigated. The drugs don't necessarily have to have been smuggled into the U.S. The jar may have contained drugs that were consumed in the country of origin; and the authorities in that country ought to be notified. But far from cooperating with law enforcement, they're trying to 'kill the messenger' - by which I mean, to sully your wife's reputation and the local dealer's reputation by calling the piece a fake.

"We don't have to fly to Seattle to know that your wife is in danger. Try to understand. You're involved in a far more vicious crime than art forgery. Have you gone to any other law enforcement authorities with this problem?"

"We tried, but no one would take the charge seriously," Maitlin insisted.

"What exactly did the DEA agents say?"

"When my wife Sylvia took the jar down to Seattle to the Drug Enforcement Agency's office, she took the dog with her. They wouldn't let her in the building with the dog and she couldn't leave the dog in the car. It was a hot day. This is a big jar in a velvet-lined box. She stamped her foot and said she wasn't leaving until someone from the DEA talked to her. Finally an agent came down to get rid of her. She told him the problem and he wanted to take the jar to have it tested. But my wife would not surrender the jar to him. So it was a bit of a fiasco. I made a few calls and an agent did go to talk to the museum people. End of story as far as the DEA was concerned."

"What kind of jar is this?"

"It's big... maybe two feet tall. The agent tried to be nice and tell her that dogs, like people, get old and senile sometimes. And maybe the dog is having a 'senior moment.' My wife did not react well. She called him a fool and contacted the dog training people and some of the men associated with the Canine Corps. They staged a demonstration using the jar and a group of other items. Max alerted to the jar and then the items were moved around to different places in the room and six other trained dogs were brought in, one at a time, and each one of them alerted to the jar."

George groaned. "She's getting herself in deeper and deeper. Did that demonstration attract attention?"

"Oh, yes. The newspeople covered it. The idea that the presence of drugs was in Max's demented mind was thoroughly discredited."

"Please listen to what I'm warning you about. The drug smugglers may fear that there is, in fact, residual - let's say - heroin in the jar. A chemical analysis of the powder will tell law enforcement where the heroin was processed. Each processor has his own chemical 'signature,' and to determine that point of origin will help to determine the steps in its distribution. This isn't street-level information; it's at the vital international shipping level. The drug supplier and shippers will not want that source to be known. They won't want any law-enforcement agency to get a hold of that jar. Also, for all you know, there's a reason that the jar fell into civilian hands. Some mistake or other might have been made by the shipper, but more than likely it was made at the consignee's end. People get reckless when they try to cover up a mistake. Your wife is in danger. Do you understand what I'm trying to tell you?"

"Yes. Yes. I understand," Maitlin said in such a tone that George knew he did not understand anything that he had been told.

"Mr. Maitlin, drug traffickers are vicious people. Are you sure that this is not an open police case?"

"I assure you, it is not. We've gone to the local police and to the offices of the DEA. Nobody is interested in what my dog smells. My wife is being made a laughingstock because she purchased a jar that she says is a genuine antique and the museum insists that it is not."

"Explain then - if they sold it as genuine and now they say it's fake, why hasn't the dealer been involved. Shouldn't somebody be getting a refund of a purchase price?"

"Under normal conditions, the buyer would take it back to the dealer and the dealer would take it back to the museum. We're not dealing with 'normal' here. My wife paid $30,000 for that jar and she says it is an absolute steal at that price. My wife says that it is genuine. She's not going to return it to anyone."

George groaned again. "My associate tells me that you want us there on Monday. What is happening on Monday?"

"An art expert is flying in from Honolulu on Monday. He'll examine the piece and give his opinion. We'd like our own investigators to be there just to beef-up our position that we're serious about establishing the truth."

"This will be an expensive 'beefing-up' function. You do realize that we'll need a contract signed and a twenty thousand dollar retainer paid up front. We'll give you a full accounting and refund to you any monies not spent. This means that you'll have to meet us at SeaTac to conduct the business end of things."

"Yes, of course, I'll be there. What should I do about my wife?"

"I know enough about women to know that telling you to gag her and tie her to a chair won't work. They're too smart for the direct approach. There's got to be an exhibit or something down in San Francisco or someplace. Call the Chamber of Commerce in San Francisco. Maybe somebody's got a vase she can authenticate... think of something to get her out of the house until Monday morning. With any luck, your house will be burglarized over the weekend while you're away and the thieves will get the jar. In other words, they won't have to kill you and your wife to get it. Give the servants a couple of days off."

Maitlin suddenly affected a cavalier attitude. "I appreciate your concern, Wagner, but I think you're exaggerating the danger just a bit." He then laughed in a more good-natured way. "If she thought for one minute that someone would break in while she was away, she'd never leave the house. This is no ordinary jar to her. It is identical to one that was in her family for several generations. It has sentimental value... which, I'm sure you know, means more than commercial value. I'll see to it that she stays quiet for the next few days. Can you get here by Sunday afternoon?"

"Let me have Sensei Wong make reservations... give us a minute."

Sensei made the reservations. "American Airlines, e.t.a. 1:10 p.m."

George added, "We'll have contracts with us that you can sign at the airport. We can't proceed with the case unless all the relevant documents are executed."

"That," said Maitlin emphatically, "is something a businessman understands. Is there anything else I should do?"

"Explain to your wife and your servants that if anyone tries to burglarize the house, they shouldn't try to be heroic. Just let the thieves take the jar."

"I'll pass the information along although I still think you're much too concerned about that jar. Well, you're the professional. I'll try to keep Sylvia quiet which won't be easy since she regards her voice as a voice for justice."

George laughed. "Without women we would not be civilized."

"And that's bad?" Maitlin laughed and ended the call.

SUNDAY, SEPTEMBER 11, 2011

Terrell Maitlin showed a more relaxed state of mind when he stood at the gate and watched the passengers deplane. As a joke, he waved a ballpoint pen and a cashier's check. After George and Sensei presented their identification, he said, "Come into my office," and indicated that they should sit at the end row of waiting-room seats.

"You seem to be in an upbeat mood," George noted.

"Gentlemen," Maitlin confided, "God has blessed me with a nose and throat structure such that I do not snore. I am so well rested. After I talked to you I realized that it would be easier to get my wife out of town than it would be to shut her up about that damned jar. I talked to a friend of mine and, as luck would have it, he had two empty chairs in his opera box in San Francisco for a Saturday night performance of some new opera, *Heart of a Soldier*. This meant that my wife had to rush out and buy a new gown and wrap, and she had to schedule an appointment at the hotel beauty parlor down there. You've gotta look good when you're sitting in someone's box. I was so relieved after talking to you that I relaxed and slept through the whole thing. I'm sort of tone-deaf. Music's not my thing. But Sylvia loves it and was happy that I didn't make any noise. Then we had a nice dinner and too much champagne and slept until ten. We just got home an hour ago. The servants said there was no disturbance of any kind at the house."

As they drove north to his home, Maitlin discussed in more detail the peculiar circumstances of the jar's purchase and provenance. "As I told you, my wife regards herself as an authority on antique Chinese porcelain artworks--"

Before he could continue, George interrupted him. "Is she in fact an expert?"

9

Maitlin did not know how to answer. "I don't know. Only experts are qualified to make that judgment. I'm not an expert."

"That's the problem," George said. "Descriptions of ability that begin with 'regards himself as an expert' are usually prejudicial. To keep an unbiased view of the facts of the case, we have to keep the playing field level. In other words, she regards herself as an expert, but she is not necessarily regarded as an expert by persons who regard themselves as experts."

Maitlin grinned. "You know... I should be looking at the problem more from my wife's point of view. I'm glad you qualified the term. I've been unfair to her." He drove in silence for a few minutes. "Let me tell you about a lesson I thought I learned but obviously forgot. There's a small museum north of here... near the Canadian border. Twenty years or so ago, the museum acquired a piece of porcelain that was supposed to be nearly six hundred years old. It was said to be a Yongle... or something... Emperor's bowl. It was from the Imperial kitchen or dining room. The museum curator declared it to be a genuine piece of early Ming porcelain. Other experts said that it was a fake. My wife was permitted to examine it and she agreed with the museum expert and pronounced it an authentic piece. But this was late in the 1980's post 'Ping Pong' diplomacy phase, and anything that had to do with China was politically 'delicate.' Soon there was an expert behind every tree in the forest, and most of them declared the bowl to be fake. My wife - in her own outspoken way - said, 'Like hell it is. That piece is genuine.' People laughed at her and then, when experts from both Red China and Taiwan claimed it was fake, the museum curator was disgraced.

"The Chinese take their reputations very seriously. No room for error. The curator had resigned in complete humiliation. Not my wife. She was so convinced about her abilities that she remained absolutely calm about the whole fiasco. I was stupid enough to be embarrassed, but you know how it is... the men at my club had wives who fancied themselves to be experts at all sorts of things. They gave me their sympathy, and I reacted by developing a patronizing attitude towards her. Then the museum sold the piece for a modest sum... as an excellent copy of a genuine bowl.

"And the next thing we heard was from an old intelligence officer who had defected back in the pre-Nixon era. He found the whole incident amusing. He explained that the whole problem was based on politics. When the Nationalist Chinese lost the civil war and retreated to Taiwan, they removed many art treasures from Chinese museums and put the pieces on display in Taipei. Years later, this particular bowl had been stolen from the Taipei museum and turned up in that small museum which is where my wife examined it. The Red Chinese wanted it back and the Taiwanese didn't want them to have it or to admit that their security had been lax. There were so many 'secret agent' art experts who gave their opinions that the controversy, itself, devalued the piece. The piece was quietly sold and then we learned that it was back in China and on display in a museum as a genuine Yongle bowl. This news was barely noticed, locally. I don't know what happened to that curator, but I do know that nobody came around to my wife Sylvia to let her say, 'I told you it was authentic.' I should have knocked a few heads together. Well, I won't make that mistake again. She says the damned ginger jar is genuine. And I don't know what my dog smells that can turn it into a fake!"

Terrell Maitlin pulled into his driveway and parked near the portico.

There was nothing modest about the police commissioner's home. It sat alone on a small hilltop, laid out in a north-south line that let it capture the morning sun on one side and the afternoon sun on the other. Viewed from either side, it appeared to be a much larger house than it was.

Maitlin led them through the front doorway and said, "My grandmother wanted to name this house 'Rosebox' because it was shaped like one of those long boxes that they deliver roses in. My grandfather called it 'Yardstick.' She didn't like that so it never got a name."

With the exception of the entrance hall, the long building was only two-rooms' deep. A hallway ran down its midline, with rooms on either side - the doors to which were now closed, giving the floor a hotel corridor feeling. "We raised three children in this house," Maitlin explained. "Both my parents and grandparents raised five kids in this house. They believed in 'compartmentalized' space, which does have its merits. One kid studies piano, but another kid plays the guitar. So we have two soundproof music rooms. The man of the house has a 'man-cave' as they now call it, and the lady of the house has a hobby room. Upstairs are the bedrooms and down here also are the kitchen, library, dining room, and, of course, the living room which is also my wife's porcelain gallery."

The door to the living room was secured with an electronic combination lock. Maitlin punched the keys in the required sequence and the lock clicked. He pushed the door open and ushered them into the sitting room gallery. A dozen cabinets, containing crisscrossing wires and paddings, displayed the fragile pieces of antique Chinese ceramics around the periphery of the room, while upholstered chairs formed a semi-circle around a low table in front of the fireplace. "Please make yourselves comfortable," he said.

Maitlin returned to the foyer and called up a stairwell, "Honey! Can you come down here and bring that Qing ginger jar with you that some of those museum quacks are calling a 'fake.' I've got some people here who are going to prove you right!"

George and Sensei looked around, noticing the steel bars on the windows. They were crossed diagonally and formed diamond shapes that were inlaid with beveled crystal panes. The interior windows were casement style panels that opened inwards. Maitlin noticed their interest in the windows. "The casement windows open only to allow for cleaning the inside of the permanent security screen. The room is sealed and contains materials that have all been 'fireproof treated.' All of the wood that once framed this section of the house, including the ceiling, was replaced by steel and the original plaster lath was replaced with fireproof panels. Ceramic tile floor on the concrete. The room is more like a steel cage than any prison cell you can find. The artworks are held in place by wires and secured in their bases with padding. The glass is unbreakable glass - similar to what is in the windows of a presidential limousine. If you tipped a cabinet over, not only wouldn't the glass break, but the pieces inside would not move. We have frequent tremors in this part of the country, so this kind of earthquake protection is needed. There's nothing in here… no rug nor upholstery… that can give off toxic fumes.

The collection is safe in here. It's not a panic room, but it's close to being one. That door we entered is steel. It looks like wood, but it's steel - as are the baseboards and wainscoting."

George said, "Very nice," but he thought it probably gave them a false sense of security. The only thing needed to open the room was a knife to someone's throat. The earthquake and fire safety measures, on the other hand, were remarkable. As he walked around the room with Sensei, looking at the pieces and reading their presentation labels, Sensei nudged him and whispered, "I did a little research before we arrived. This collection is probably worth many millions. I'm amazed."

Maitlin called his houseboy on the intercom. "Put Max on a leash and bring him in here. On your way out, tell cook to serve us tea and sandwiches in here."

Sylvia Maitlin had taken her time getting ready to meet their guests. She finally called down, "Are you restraining the dog, Terry?"

"Yes, my love. Max is on one end of the leash and I am on the other." Everyone looked at Max who sat upright at Maitlin's feet, his ears up, his mouth a little open, and his tail contentedly thumping the carpet.

Sylvia Maitlin was a petite woman whose voice had the clear certitude that added another foot to her height and thirty pounds to her weight. She was pretty and dressed in a youthful casual style. Her hair was bleached a dark blonde color which she wore in a page-boy style. She was not what George and Sensei had expected.

She entered the room carrying a large wooden box that looked as though it could hold two or three stacked breadboxes. As soon as she opened the box and removed the jar from its velvet-lined styrofoam interior, she took the lid off the jar, and the dog began to pull on the leash, trying to get to the piece of porcelain. Maitlin let the dog guide him to the jar; and the dog, while making a soft growling noise, sat in an "alert" stance beside it, indicating that it smelled an illegal drug. "Do you see?" Sylvia asked the detectives. "This is the exact condition in which I purchased this jar. I have not washed it. I have examined it, and it is authentic and quite beautiful."

George and Sensei agreed that the jar was beautiful. "Will you allow us to take photographs of it so that we can discover how this beautiful thing got involved in the drug trade?" George asked.

Sylvia corrected George by mouthing the word "jar" for him to use in place of "thing." She smiled. "You'll need to get clear photos of its bottom... in Chinese porcelain that would be 'the money shot.' Come on outside. The light is better." George followed her out onto the portico. Increasingly, as she posed and handled the jar in a light-hearted way, he understood her husband's devotion.

George took more than a dozen shots of the jar. When they returned to the living room, she went upstairs and returned with a stack of other photographs. "You can add them to your collection," she said. "Most of them are official... copyrighted shots. Now you have your own, too. Although I'm having difficulty convincing people, the piece is nearly a hundred and fifty years old. There are not many of these jars left. They're too big to sit on a table, and they have domed lids so they can't function as tables, either. It's true! Some jars have wide flat lids, and people actually use them as end tables. So these just sit on the floor with nothing to do but get knocked about and broken. But in dynastic times, such a jar would grace the dining room of an emperor."

"Your husband," said George, "regards you as the Oracle of oriental porcelain. If you say it is genuine, he assured us, then it is genuine. It must be nice to have someone believe in your abilities as much as your husband believes in yours. Now... if we talk about my ex-wife and her opinions about me and my abilities..."

The remark was appreciated by Terrell Maitlin. He ordered more tea and asked the houseboy to take Max outside to the back yard. Sylvia enthusiastically ordered that rooms be prepared for their guests. "Somebody is on my side," she murmured, looking at George. "I ought to hire an orchestra for the event." She turned to Sensei, "Sifu... are you a vegetarian?"

"Only when I have to be," Sensei replied.

"And George?"

"Only when our partner Beryl is around," George allowed. "She is the divine enemy of arterial plaque."

Sylvia made a thumb's up sign of approval and then went into the kitchen to give instructions to the cook. When she returned she led everyone through a tour of the downstairs of the house.

A few fundamental beliefs governed Sylvia Maitlin's attitude towards life. She fervently believed that formal education was worthless if it were not accompanied by experience. Her hobby room was filled with tools... carpenter's, plumber's, potter's. She had vises and mountings that secured handsaws, both rip and crosscut, and she had the correct files to use to sharpen them. All that a pioneer could hope to have, she had. Planes, chisels, drills... but nothing electric. She had a potters' wheel which she made from a truck's wheel rim. She did not use any of these tools expertly, but just enough to know their value and to be able to appreciate a piece of furniture for the way it was crafted.

According to her philosophy, objects of study that could not be experienced - as for example, a walk on the lunar surface, still had to have an experiential reference if they were to be imagined - otherwise they would have no more significance than a fairy tale. The principles of flight she taught by giving her children lessons in gliding and parachuting. All three of them were licensed small craft pilots. She took them camping in Death Valley and in the Northwest's woods. They could "sing along" with the major arias from all the great operas before they cut their wisdom teeth. They also knew a Rubens from a Rembrandt.

Sitting again in the living room, they began to talk casually about many subjects, and George, who had once feared that he would dislike the determined Sylvia Maitlin, found himself enjoying her company. "She's like Scheherazade," he said, "a one-woman entertainment industry."

Maitlin smiled at her. He was as captivated by his wife in her forties as he had been when she was a teenager. He discussed her while she was sitting in front of them. "Let me tell you about this woman," he said. "Some people have been foolish enough to call her a 'Jack of all trades, master of none' because her interests have been so diverse. As a child she had enjoyed mountain climbing; and when, as an adult, a group of our friends planned to scale Denali, they denied her a position - because, they said, 'she wasn't sufficiently experienced and couldn't pull her share in an emergency.' What does she do? She trains fanatically, turns her charm on a few people, and secures a position in a small expedition to Antarctica. She never boasted about the excursion or engaged in any one-upmanship with the Denali climbers. But she still displays an ordinary Mason jar of melted Antarctic snow prominently on the table in the foyer beside a delicate Nymphenburg Comedia dell Arte porcelain acrobat. Everyone who sees it has to ask. If she owned a half dozen Faberge eggs, she'd form a semi-circle of them and put that damned Mason jar right up front in the middle. So, we can't underestimate her confidence in this Chinese ginger jar."

Sylvia had placed the jar on a table and George got up to look at it. To him, it was just a pretty drug container, and it was time to discuss it. "For some reason I imagined that it would be smaller. This one could hold ten or fifteen pounds of coffee beans. Tell us how you happened to buy it."

"George, I don't expect you to understand this, but collecting is an addiction. I'm an addict. I see something I like and then a chemical reaction occurs in my brain and I begin to crave the thing. I see it. I want it. I need it. I go crazy if I can't get it. It's all I can think about.

"Technically," she said, "it is an Imperial Qing Dynasty jar, made during the reign of the Guangxu Emperor Zaitian. I date it to be precisely made in 1880. The term 'ginger jar' is an all purpose name for any storage jar with a lid. It can hold a pint, a quart, a gallon, five gallons. The vast majority of jars of this size were made for kitchen use. Not that many were made for a function in the Emperor's dining room. This one should have a teak wood base. I'll get one when I finally am able to display the piece." She pointed at a corner. "I'll put it on a pedestal right over there. Standing on its base it would be maybe twenty inches tall."

"How can you date it so specifically?" Sensei asked.

"My great grandfather was a graduate of the Jefferson Medical College in Philadelphia. He fell madly in love with a woman from Seattle and wanted to join her here. Traveling across country was not cheap and the solution to the money problem came by answering an advertisement. A rich family who had several sickly members was making a journey across country on the new Transcontinental railroad, and they wanted a physician to be with them at all times. That was in 1873.

"He reached San Francisco and concluded his service with the family. He booked passage on a ship that was due to sail for Seattle in a few days' time, and as he happily walked along the dock, carrying everything he owned, he was suddenly mugged. The next thing he knew he was locked in the hold of a merchant ship that was bound, quite literally, for Shanghai. Yes," she laughed, "he was shanghaied to Shanghai! Fortunately, they had thrown his suitcase and medical bag down into the hold with him.

"His medical skill became his salvation. When they reached Shanghai, he was asked to attend a member of an English family. He cured the patient - I don't know what was wrong or what he did, but he quickly established himself as a fine physician; and word of his abilities reached the court in Beijing. So he was living well in China. He wrote to the woman in Seattle, who became my great grandmother, and she went to China. He learned Mandarin and one day he was summoned to the Imperial Court to care for a girl who was somehow related to the royal family. Her feet had been bound and her foot had gotten infected. He stayed with her until her foot was cured of the infection. In 1880 the Empress, as a bonus for his service to the girl, gave him a big jar. I have a grainy photo of it. It's an identical twin to this jar. This has the same imperial kiln mark, the same six linear Chinese characters in the 'reign identification' written by the same scribe, the same five-claw dragon motif, and the same colored under-glazing and gilded finishing on the basal rim and lid. When my great-grandfather received his jar, he was told it was from a new batch of dishes that had just been delivered to court. He brought the jar with him when he fled China at the turn of the century. Those were the Boxer Rebellion days. He practiced medicine here.

"The jar was passed down to my grandfather who taught chemistry here in the University and also in Hong Kong. He lived in China until the Japanese invaded in the late 1930's. He came home here and married. My father was born here but he went to Oxford to get a degree in Chinese culture. He, too, lived in Hong Kong during the Cultural Revolution. He returned here, married, and I was born here in 1968. I never went to college but I grew up immersed in the mystique of the Flying Tigers and a knowledge of writing Chinese in the old style. I was not an adept, but what is more important is that the writing I was most familiar with was the Imperial style and vocabulary used as identifying marks on porcelains and on diplomatic gifts and such. Some of my collection came from my great-grandfather; some from my grandfather; but most of it came from my father who brought dozens of pieces back from Hong Kong - pieces he obtained with a scholar's eye. I knew Chinese porcelain. He'd take me to museums all over the U.S. and Canada. But the ginger jar was special.

"I saw that jar every day of my life until my father broke it into a thousand pieces when he collapsed of a fatal heart attack in 1988. It was as if he was reaching out to it for support as he fell. It could not be repaired.

"When I saw this jar and Ezra Zhen wanted only thirty-thousand dollars for it, I was thrilled. But to be honest, I felt a little insulted that he only wanted thirty thousand dollars for it. I actually protested, 'But Ezra! It is worth so much more!' I don't know why he let me have it so cheaply. He knew the story of my great grandfather's acquisition of the jar. Or, maybe he thought I was mistaken. I don't know. I had to have it. It was a craving I had to satisfy."

"It's beautiful," said George. "I understand your addiction."

"You're a collector?" she asked incredulously.

"No, not the porcelain, just the addiction. I was shot in my knee and also in a particularly painful nerve center in my shoulder. After a year of non-stop surgery, I was addicted to morphine and needed another year in rehab."

The rays of the afternoon sun shone directly onto the jar, imbuing it with an other-worldly sheen. Sensei imagined that if a person stared at it long enough, it would act like a yantra and draw the person into a deep state of meditation.

"I suppose," George continued, "that an addiction to satisfy a collector's craving must be as hard to break as kicking opiates. This, at least, is beautiful. There's nothing beautiful about narcotics when they're causing the pain they were designed to relieve."

"Yes," she replied. "Now you need to be cured of the cure. In the disease of collecting, it doesn't take long before the thrill of the new piece wears off and you need to get another one. A 'bowl fix.' A 'vase fix.' I guess there's no other way to look at it. A collector is an addict. I don't care who disagrees. We are addicts. It can be so destructive. I know a man who spent his children's college money on a piece of porcelain that turned out to be a fake. It destroyed the family. It was still an exquisite piece of porcelain; but that is not enough to satisfy the need of a collector. Rarity and history matter more than beauty. My husband knew a family that spent a fortune on methamphetamine addiction cures for their son. After they went bankrupt, he went into the underground. They don't even know if he's dead or alive. When I told Terrell I wanted this jar, he said, 'Get it if you want it. At least we can look at it and smile.' That's the kind of man my husband is."

"So when and where did you see the piece?" George asked. "Give us all the details and leave nothing out."

"First you should be taken up to your room. The servants can bring your luggage. You can freshen up and put some comfortable clothing on. We have wonderful cashmere and cotton-blended yoga clothing... all sizes. Terry will take you up and get you the right size with slippers, too... I'll also put on my "cashmere scrubs" I call them. In another hour dinner will be served and then I'll tell you everything."

After they finished dinner - during which no mention of porcelain was made - Sylvia Maitlin instructed the houseboy to serve coffee on the roof. She led the three men up a circular staircase that delivered them to a "sitting area" on the roof. The kitchen maid had gone ahead to set up folding chairs and small tables so that they could relax and admire the view of the ocean in front of them or turn around and see an unobstructed view of the mountains.

The setting sun divided the Pacific with a golden path that led straight to the horizon. Louvered catamarans and sailboats skimmed across the water, their sails' edges gilded with light. Billowing white clouds formed as they neared the shore and drifted over the land in no hurry to collide with the Cascade Mountains, while groves of pine trees stood sentinel down the hillside, giving off their scent which the sea breeze carried to the rooftop. "It's beautiful up here," Sensei said. "Do you come up here often?"

"No," Sylvia said. "This part of the roof was specially built to accommodate people. Every now and then I do come up to check things. I don't enjoy it. I get an uneasy feeling and I'm always relieved to get back down. But the view is spectacular and I thought you'd enjoy it." After another minute of watching the ocean, she began to tell them how she had acquired the ginger jar.

"I got the piece from Ezra Zhen, an antique dealer here in town I know well. He also repairs broken porcelains. I've had nothing but good luck dealing with him. His shop is small - the downstairs of a three storey building. I think he lives in the back room, but I can't say for sure. He has a workroom, a storage room that I think he often sleeps in, and a kitchen; but his showroom is small. His pieces are exquisite. He told me that he once had a Han bowl that now is worth a million."

"Why do you specify some porcelain as 'Imperial'?" George asked.

"Porcelain made for the royal household is very valuable. It is superior in every way to the porcelains produced for non-royal consumers. Of course, the market has been virtually destroyed by all the fakes."

"An application of Gresham's law?" Sensei asked.

"If it were only that. But it's more than just the fake driving the real out of circulation. The market is so corrupted by unscrupulous dealers and unqualified experts, that nobody is quite sure which piece is authentic and therefore more valuable and should be 'hoarded.' The jar is worth considerably more than the thirty thousand we paid for it. But that's what Ezra wanted for it. I know, I know. I should have married for money and not for love," she said, winking at her husband.

"Why didn't the museum curator or the dealer know that it was worth more?" Sensei asked.

"I have no idea. Every conceivable possibility has gone through my mind. It makes no sense. One day, Ezra called me to tell me that the museum had negotiated for several jars from a very reputable dealer with offices in Singapore and Bangkok. The Smith-Cheung Galleries. They had been assured that the museum would be receiving a large donation from someone's estate; but then the will was challenged, and the money was not forthcoming 'in a timely manner' as we say. So they could not afford all the pieces. Ezra happened to be in the museum as the crates were being delivered. He knew I had a weakness for large Qing jars, and he also knew that it was a buyer's market. The museum needed the money to reimburse the seller in Singapore. He bid on several pieces and his bids were accepted.

"These pieces are fragile and as such are sometimes packed in the same stuff they test bullets in - ballistics gelatin - maybe it has another ingredient or two... but it's essentially the same. Only in this case they put a thin rubber collar around the jar's neck before they put the lid on, and then they smear the whole piece in a Vaseline-type coating, bag it in a clear plastic baggie, and submerge it in a square of lukewarm gel that's set inside a big clear plastic bag... and then let the gel congeal around it. The gel does melt, but not as easily as dessert gelatin. It's much more solid. You could drop that plastic bag onto the surface of Mars from one of those parachute things and it would bounce and bounce and nothing would harm the porcelain. The gel absorbs all the impact. They put the square plastic bag in a styrofoam container that fits perfectly inside a wooden crate, and ship it. A piece like this particular ginger jar is shipped in a crate that is nearly a meter square.

"The whole - apparently unopened - crate was delivered to his shop. He turned his workroom into a kind of sauna and he put the gelatin-encased jar in a mesh hammock over a large tub... and let it sit there and slowly the gel did soften and melt away, sliding down into the tub. He told me that the gelatin is reusable.

"I was in the shop just as the melting period was nearing the end and he and I witnessed the falling away of the last blob of gel. Then he carefully removed the jar from its clear plastic baggie. He wrapped a towel around the jar and carried it into his display room. Together we sat on either side of the counter and with fine Egyptian cotton we wiped away the oily coating. I was in love. I literally wept looking at this jar.

I called my husband and he could hear the desire in my voice. 'Get it, Hon,' he said. So I wrote a check right on the spot and gave it to Ezra. He created the box for it. He cutout some styrofoam and covered it with velvet and I put the jar inside it and brought it home. The dog went crazy trying to sit in front of it. He was alerting!

"Right away I said, 'This jar has something to do with narcotics.' But I knew it could not have been Ezra Zhen's doing. I was there when he melted away the shipping gel. So it was between the dealer and the museum. I'll let Terry tell you what he did."

Terrell Maitlin pursed his lips and whistled. "I reported it and became a pariah. The Singapore police are fanatical about eliminating drug trafficking of any kind. Was I trying to make them look incompetent? Oh, boy! And then... everybody's so sick of hearing about Chinese fake art in Vancouver and Seattle. And here I was with a new scandal... involving drugs yet! The museum people here were furious with my wife and me for attempting to slander them. My wife will not allow anyone to take the jar out of her possession without a warrant. The dog's nose did not constitute a reasonable cause to seize her property - especially since the jar was empty.

"So then the museum people said that the piece was obviously a fake that had been created by the sort of low-life criminals who create art fakes. Since they hadn't opened the crate, they couldn't even be sure it was the same jar. As the museum curator said, 'The crook who created this fake obviously had drugs on his hands and this is what the dog smelled.' Then he tried to get funny. 'The dog refuses to tell us whether he smelled opium or marijuana, and since the jar is quite empty, I'm afraid we'll never know the details of what his canine nose detected.' He insisted that the crate had not been opened by the museum's receiving room. Essentially, it went from the dock to Ezra's shop... as far as they're concerned. Dr. Gao slammed Ezra by saying, 'Reputable dealers would have handled the piece with latex gloves.' And that was that. Once again, my wife was regarded as a dupe of some kind, a silly woman who got tricked into spending a lot of money on a fake just because, as one of them put it, 'She considers herself an expert'."

"Tell them what Gao, one of the museum experts, said about testing," Sylvia pouted.

"My wife agreed to have the piece tested using the Thermoluminescence procedure. Doctor Gao laughed at her and said that they scrape off old glazes and put them in new glazes and easily fool the test. Then he went on to explain that fakers will let the piece sit in sewer water for weeks - which he thought was most likely with this piece - to give it 'an antique look.' How's that for denigrating the piece? A shit patina! He also allowed that it was possible that there were drugs in my house - possibly a servant's - and that in handling the drugs and the jar we had given the dog all he needed to smell."

George looked puzzled. "I've got a question about the shipping method. Why don't they ship the porcelains in those peanut styrofoam things? Those things protect an object very well. Why go to all that trouble?"

"About ten years ago," Sylvia calculated, "there was a large shipment of genuine antique porcelain pieces shipped in those styrofoam peanuts and there was a fire on board the ship and the peanuts melted onto the porcelain. That stuff turns black and tar-like. But you can get tar off. Apparently the melted styrofoam they use just fuses to something, and in the attempt to get it off, the pieces were damaged badly. I know that gelatin can melt in the heat but it won't damage the jar, and the jar is just supposed to float in it."

"Ok. Now I understand. Let's get back to the gel removal. You saw the gelatin. Was it clear and clean?"

"I could see that there were flecks of debris in it. It was tinted that pale beige color you get when you dissolve Knox gelatin. Ezra had said that the gel could be reused. I guess it could contain debris from wherever it was used before."

Terrell Maitlin was not inclined to consider clues about packing or shipping. "Gel?" he asked derisively. "What the jar was packed in is not nearly so important as finding out what was packed in the jar. Find out why the dog alerts to the piece and it will be worth any expense."

Sensei ignored his comment. "Where does that leave things now? Is anyone investigating you?"

"It's all at the gossip stage," Maitlin answered. "There's been no official investigation. However, at the museum director's insistence, an expert from Honolulu is being brought in here tomorrow. That's why I wanted you here before Monday. This expert is going to give his opinion on the jar's authenticity. My wife has agreed to let him examine it in her presence."

"So," George said, "if the piece is determined to be a fake, the presence of drugs is easily understood. But what happens if he decides that the piece is genuine?"

"Then," said Maitlin, "they'll say that the dirty hands were either in the dealer's shipping room or in this house."

"Let's back up a minute," George said. "Wouldn't importing fake artifacts involve customs or some other law enforcement agency? Selling fake art as genuine is fraud. Crimes have been committed. Why isn't a fake jar evidence of a crime?"

"Crime?" Maitlin asked. "Who's going to file the charge? My wife paid the money and she says it's genuine."

Pleading fatigue, George retired before the others and called Beryl. The three-hour time difference would have her getting ready for bed while he was having dinner. As it was, she was watching TV in her apartment above the office.

"I'm going to send you photographs of the jar," he said. "Wish me luck with this electronic stuff."

Beryl whistled as the pictures came in on her laptop. "You've taken great shots."

"Can you show them to that curator down at the Art Museum? I know Imperial Chinese porcelain isn't his specific subject, but maybe he can discreetly ask the correct expert what he can tell him about the piece. This is clearly a drug case - not a case about art, although the art obviously has something to do with it."

"I'll print these out on glossy paper in the morning and show them to Doug down at the Museum."

MONDAY, SEPTEMBER 12, 2011

Ezra Zhen, short, round, and bespectacled, had a horrified expression on his face. It was as if the four adults who entered his small shop constituted a mob. Two he knew, but two were strangers and he could not watch all of them at once.

George handed him his card. Zhen looked at it and asked, "What are you investigating?"

"We're trying to discover why some people in the art scene around here are trying to smear your reputation... yours and Mrs. Maitlin's."

Zhen sighed. "Nothing like this has ever happened to me before," he said, shaking his head. "I unpacked that porcelain jar and wiped it with cotton. I saw it as closely as a person can see it. I know a real antique from a phony one. So does Mrs. Maitlin. Are you folks on your way to the Museum's 'big reveal' - the test by a real expert - since nobody considers us experts? My car is in the shop. Do you have room in yours for me?"

"Of course," Maitlin said. "Let's go together and present a united front. But first we have to take these two gentlemen down to SeaTac and wait while they welcome a 'real' expert."

Sensei pointed to a blue and white ginger jar. "My father had one like that. Fish and flowers. He said it was valuable. He sold it when he made his big, but aborted, move to China."

"If the jar was in mint condition and it was of this dynasty, he would have made a lot of money - assuming he sold it to someone reputable."

"How much would you say?"

"It depends on when he sold it. Today it might bring a million or so."

George nudged Sensei. "No wonder you don't like Chinese food."

As they waited at the gate, a scholarly Chinese gentleman stood erect holding a sign that said, "Kalahele." George nudged Sensei. "That must be Doctor Peng from the Museum. George and Sensei instantly spotted Herbert Kalahele as he came through the jetway, but Doctor Peng did not seem to recognize the man despite the fact that he was wearing a bright flowered Hawaiian shirt and carrying luggage that consisted of four reference books taped to a small clear plastic bag that held a folded Hawaiian shirt, briefs, and a pair of socks. George and Sensei went up to him and introduced themselves and pointed out Doctor Peng who was still looking for someone who would read his sign.

To George, it was immediately apparent that something was wrong. Kalahele had no other clothing with him and not only were his carry-on items peculiarly packed, but he would have to be in a distracted state to enter the Seattle area in the middle of September and be dressed for tropical weather. A cold rain had fallen overnight and the temperature had dropped. Kalahele was shivering a minute after he left the gate. After shaking hands with Doctor Peng, he said, simply, "Can we get started for the museum?"

As they walked towards the exit, George noticed also that his movements were jerky, his gaze darted from side to side, and he seemed not to be focused on where he was going. When spoken to, he responded in a polite, professional way, but George could tell that he was experiencing considerable anxiety.

George knew that he couldn't help whatever was bothering the Hawaiian at the moment, but he could alleviate the man's shivering. As they passed a Seattle Seahawks' sportswear shop in the mall, he stopped, saying that he wanted to buy shirts for his fourteen year-old son and nearly twelve year-old daughter. He bought three: a medium for his boy, a small for his daughter, and an extra large for Kalahele who murmured, "Thank you" and put it on.

In the airport parking lot, they parted company: Kalahele went with Doctor Peng to the museum, while Sensei and George walked to the Maitlin's car where Zhen, Sylvia and Terrell sat waiting. Everyone had already agreed to rendezvous at the museum in half an hour.

Before they got into the car, George quietly asked Sensei, "Can you call Jake in Honolulu? Kalahele is scared."

The one-storey museum looked like the square Dao temples Sensei had seen in Taiwan. The hipped-style roof was made of glazed aquamarine ceramic tiles that sloped and curved, overhanging the sides. The eaves upturned gracefully and all the centerlines supported animal figurines - monkeys, ducks, dragons, lions, and puppies - that played atop the four seams that converged at a center pearl-ball.

Beside the front revolving door, a banner written both in Chinese calligraphy and in English print announced that the museum was exhibiting a small collection of antique Japanese ceramics. "If we have time," Sensei whispered, "I'd like to have a look at that." As they passed through the doors, however, he headed for the relative privacy of the men's room and called Jake Renquist in Honolulu.

Years before, in Taiwan, Jake and Sensei found themselves to be the only Americans in two separate martial arts' schools, and, in what was surprising, neither school was Chinese. Renquist was studying Vajra Mushti, the Indian martial art, in a little known mountain area near Kaohsiung that had been settled by people from India centuries before. Sensei was studying Karate in Kaohsiung, in a dojo that was near the small temple and monastery in which he had been ordained. They met and, with ex-pat affinity, began to observe American holidays together with more enthusiasm than they would have felt at home: Memorial Day's Indy 500, July Fourth's baseball, October's World Series and NFL and AFC games, Halloween, Thanksgiving, Christmas, the Playoffs, and, to them, the biggest national holiday of all, the Superbowl.

Jake had a P.I. license, but he mostly attended to two jobs: he was a martial arts' instructor with the Honolulu Police Department and a public relations' agent for the Chamber of Commerce. He often traveled and whenever he was on the East coast, he would try to meet Sensei to share a meal. They spoke regularly and often asked each other for advice or for assistance in solving a variety of problems. Jake funneled information to the HPD in exchange for using its forensic data banks.

Whenever possible, the two friends would spar on "the mat," laughing at each other's attempts to use their different techniques against each other. The practice, they said, fine-tuned their own "game."

Now, in the museum's men's room, Sensei asked for help with the Herbert Kalahele "situation."

"I've heard the name," Jake said. "But I can't place him." As he spoke he did a net search and then was able to recall him. He gave a physical description of Kalahele. It matched the man who was now setting up a table in the museum's entrance hall. "The guy is an expert on Chinese porcelains," he read, glancing at the biographical information. "He worked for a Chinese antique dealer when he was a kid... then he studied the chemistry of ceramics at the U of Hawaii and Chinese archeology and dynastic history... he's got a master's degree. What's he doing in Seattle?"

"There's something funny going on. He's here to judge the authenticity of a piece of porcelain... a big Qing dynasty ginger jar. A client of ours bought the jar and insists it is genuine, but her dog, an old retired drug-sniffing dog, alerts to the jar. The jar had been shipped from Smith-Cheung Antiques in Singapore to the local museum. It allegedly had not been uncrated at the museum since some financial reverses forced them to sell it and several other pieces.

"After questions were raised about drugs, the museum authorities insisted that the jar was obviously a fake and the drug smell came on it when the low-life art forgers made the copy. Kalahele is supposed to settle the question of the jar's authenticity, but he is showing unusual signs of fear and loathing. There's a backstory here. Something is going on that is making him afraid. It's 53 degrees today and he shows up wearing an Hawaiian shirt with no luggage except a plastic bag that contains another shirt and pair of socks. This guy is the top of his profession and he arrived looking like a beachcomber. Can you find out what is scaring him without giving anything away?"

"Consider it done," said Jake.

The testing table contained squares of padding, high intensity lamps, jeweler's eyepieces, micrometers and other measuring devices, an ordinary biology class microscope, cleaning compounds and tissues. A box of latex gloves was also provided. There was only one chair at the table and Herbert Kalahele immediately sat on it.

As several television cameras trained their lenses on the unorthodox but locally appreciated appearance of the Hawaiian expert, George studied Kalahele's eyes. His pupils were dilated, his eyebrows furled, and he appeared to be breathing shallowly. Then Sylvia Maitlin approached and placed the box before him on the table. She unlatched the lid, removed the ginger jar from its silk-velvet lining, and set the jar on the table before him.

Suddenly, Kalahele took a deep breath, his hazel eyes brightened and his eyebrows arched. He was looking at something beautiful and exciting... a genuine piece. He muttered something. Sylvia asked him what he had said, and he looked up, startled almost, to see her. He did not answer. He removed the lid and studied it. Then, so as not to empty anything that it might contain, he held the jar up at a forty-five degree angle and bent forward to look up and examine its base. He studied the reign marks on the bottom for a few minutes and then carefully placed the jar on one of the table's pads.

Kalahele was holding the jar so reverently, George thought, that everyone should have been convinced that he was handling a genuine piece. The Hawaiian adjusted the high-intensity lamp that had been placed on the table, put on a jeweler's eyepiece, lifted the jar again and again studied the seal on the bottom of the jar. Still holding the jar with extreme care, he looked into the cameras and said, "Well, right off the bat I see disturbing signs. *En passant*, I should mention that the piece is extremely symmetrical which gives the suggestion that the clay had been thrown onto a machine-driven potter's wheel and mechanically shaped. Not an encouraging sign. What is more important is, of course, the seal.

"Chinese characters are logograms that carry elements of meaning and basic word pronunciation. China, as you know, has twenty-nine different dialects; but while they all, to varying degrees, sound different, they are all written the same. Because of the variety of spoken languages in the Imperial eras, the meaning must be precisely conveyed and the character perfectly rendered.

"In the last half century, however, Mandarin has become the official and unifying dialect and the characters have been greatly simplified. Nevertheless, to obviate the hazards of misrepresentation which individual styles present, it is necessary to inscribe the character with a specific number and order of brush strokes. This, of course, is the reason it's often necessary to count the strokes when we search a dictionary for a character's meaning. Obviously, in the Imperial eras when the characters were far more complicated and had to be read by speakers of many dialects, precision was imperative. In all square Imperial Seals and Reign Marks the inscriptions, without exception, would have to be written in these more complicated forms.

"Now, I can see that two of the characters in the Imperial Seal mark show the simplified, that is to say, the modern version of the characters... in particular the characters Guang and Zhi. The inscription on this jar was made within the last fifty years or so. There is no need to analyze the jar beyond these obvious falsities although I will note that gross inspection suggests that the underglaze looks to be of a more modern material... the margins are held more strictly than I would expect to see in an authentic period piece.

"I will submit to Doctor Peng, the museum's curator of ceramic art and artifacts, a detailed report of my findings. I regret to say that this piece, while being extraordinarily beautiful, is not genuine. I would value it between five to seven thousand dollars. A lot of work went into it. I have no further comments. Thank you." He immediately began to gather his possessions on the table.

The disappointed news reporters wanted to question Sylvia, but she said simply, "No comment." She went to the table at which Kalahele was still standing, took the jar, and looked down at him. "I will leave you to heaven," she said as she picked up the jar's lid. The neck's protective rubber collar had been removed and the lid scraped the porcelain as she placed it on the jar. "Careful!" Kalahele hissed at her.

Sylvia Maitlin's jaw dropped. She stared at him blankly.

Herbert Kalahele did not look at her. "I'm sorry," he said, "but I have to leave now. I have a 4:30 flight to catch." He remained dour and uncommunicative. He walked up to Dr. Joseph Peng and announced, "As agreed, I'll fax the report to you as soon as I get home."

Dr. Peng produced a business card and said, "Address your invoice to the museum but be sure to put it to my attention."

Kalahele pushed through the museum's doors and, seeing a cab with its light on, signaled it. "SeaTac," he said to the driver.

Dr. Sheng Gao raised his arms and signaled the visitors. "Our own in-house expert - that's right, we really didn't need outside opinions - Dr. Joseph Peng, who recognized the fake immediately, would like to make a statement relevant to this incident. I'd say, 'Take the microphone, Joe'... but we haven't got a microphone!"

This witty remark received the applause due it, and Gao, with pointed finger and all the panache of a TV announcer heralding the advent of the star of the show, proclaimed, "Ladies and Gentlemen, without further ado, may I present Dr. Joseph Peng!"

Although the room was silent, Peng raised his hands and signaled everyone to settle down. He then used the occasion to make a startlingly political speech. "I know that there is a tendency to blame everyone except the government agencies that not only tolerate but encourage such fakery.

"Gallery owners and collectors are not to blame for this unfortunate situation. No, the people who love Chinese culture and who treasure the exquisite evidence of that culture are not to blame for wanting to purchase beautiful examples of it. The blame belongs to the government of China that sanctions these deceptions. To them such fraud is a growth industry.

"Governments that lack integrity flaunt international law and common decency. Every day the Nigerian government gladly permits thousands of emails to be sent around the world in the Spanish Prisoner swindle. Innocent people are asked for a nominal sum to help the unfortunate writer. They also encourage the fraudulent Cashier's Check scheme. In nurturing the fake Chinese art scheme, the government of China has exactly the same criminal mentality as the government of

Nigeria. China and Nigeria are the Siamese twins of fraud. So do not blame the local buyers or sellers. They are the victims. Blame the thieves that profit from these frauds. Thank you."

All attention was directed away from Ezra Zhen and Sylvia Maitlin. It was as if they were not present. Linking the governments of Nigeria and China was far more newsworthy.

Sensei went to the side of the room and called Jake Renquist in Honolulu to tell him that Kalahele was catching the 4:30 flight on his way home.

Terrell and Sylvia Maitlin, Ezra Zhen, Sensei, and George got into Maitlin's car. When all the doors had closed and Maitlin inserted the key in the ignition, he said, "What do we do now?"

"Go to a restaurant," Sylvia said. "Call it 'Putting on a brave face' if you want. To me, it may be the last time I can show myself in public."

Immediately they drove to a restaurant and were seated. Sylvia tried valiantly to eat, but her distress overwhelmed her appetite. Terrell Maitlin and Ezra Zhen ordered soup and nothing else. George and Sensei were hungry and had an enjoyable seafood dinner, despite the eyes of the others at the table that watched every bite they took. When the table was cleared for coffee and dessert, everyone drank coffee and had a small dish of ice cream.

George rang his water glass with his spoon. "Commissioner Maitlin earlier asked, 'What do we do now?' I think that the best thing we can do is to each go home and get a good night's sleep. We'll all think more clearly in the morning."

His apparent cheerfulness annoyed Terrell but left Sylvia with the same bewilderment that Kalahele had caused when he spontaneously chastised her for not being more careful handling the jar. She reached down and lifted her handbag from its place beside her chair. "Yes," she said. "Let's all go home. We can drop Ezra off on our way."

In the living room, George finally was able to speak. "First," he asked Sylvia, "do you remember what Kalahele said when he first saw the jar? He seemed to whisper something."

"Yes. I was startled by it. I thought he had said, 'Beautiful!'; but after I heard his lying mouth describe the seal, I knew I was mistaken."

"No. You weren't. There isn't a detective or a psychiatrist on the planet who didn't see the indisputable signs that Kalahele knew that he was holding a genuine piece. We have already started to investigate the cause of his false report with an associate in Honolulu. I would have tried to put your minds at ease sooner but Ezra Zhen, for all we know, is part of the scheme."

Terrell Maitlin expected his wife to protest. But she said nothing. He presented what he considered his interpretation of the issues: "My wife and I tried to probe that drug angle and got nowhere - except to leave ourselves open to criticism. The shipment was not consigned to an individual. It was consigned by a reputable dealer to a reputable museum. The DEA is not interested in my dog's nose. And as far as I'm concerned, I don't give a rat's ass about the fake Chinese art market. And I also don't give a rat's ass about the thousands of dollars my wife and Ezra Zhen just lost because some Hawaiian whispers 'beautiful' to a jar that he then says is a fake. I care that my wife's intelligence has been questioned and that her reputation has been sullied. I have to look at the situation through her eyes. Jealous people will attack her character. It is not easy to live with the mockery of nasty people."

The remarks irritated George. "What money did Ezra Zhen lose? Did he offer to return your money? He'll probably say that he respects her expertise - an expertise she insists upon - and she pronounced the piece genuine. He may not have realized it at the time she purchased it, but he surely believes it now. Kalahele was holding that piece as if it were Kamehameha's skull. Something else is going on.

"Your wife's collection remains authentic no matter what people say about it. My suggestion is to use the momentary injury to her good name to get to the more important problem of injury to her life. The drug traffickers know that the jar is worth a considerable sum. They may be angry that it was sold for a paltry thirty thousand dollars, but that's the least of it. They also fear that any residua can identify their specific product. Please understand this! They want that jar! They want to destroy the powder that is in the bottom, and they may also want the heroin shipment that it once contained. I don't know the disposition of its contents. For all we know someone made off with the contents and started the domino effect of errors that ended up with your wife's getting the jar. But make no mistake-she is in danger.

"This is my suggestion: I am going to ask Sylvia to make a personal sacrifice. It will be a difficult thing to do, but I would like her to get a phony jar that looks like the real one, and then publicly to make an impassioned plea for the restoration of integrity in the art market and to dramatize the damage fakes do, by taking a hammer and smashing the jar... right there in one of the TV studios. She can say something like 'I'm destroying the false to preserve the true.'"

Sylvia Maitlin retorted angrily. "You want me to stand before cameras and tell the world I'm incompetent? I don't think so. I've been through enough with this debacle. I've spent years of my life studying books and prowling through flea markets and estate auctions. All those wretched early days of buying pieces and going through trial and error's anxiety whenever I made a purchase!

"We have a small but wonderful collection. We planned to will it to the University so that the students would see what the ancient emperors saw on their tables... what the princes ate from... what the ladies of the court drank from. And you want me to denigrate it, to cast doubt upon its authenticity! You want me to say that I am a fool who doesn't know paste from pearl. Don't you understand that if I make such a dramatic confession I will diminish the value of this collection by diminishing my own abilities. They can say what they want about me. I don't care. But I will not be complicit in any scheme that makes a dunce of my husband and a conglomeration of worthless junk of these exquisite pieces."

Terrell Maitlin agreed with his wife. "Do you know what would happen if Sylvia did what you suggest? The so-called experts would swoop down and declare her collection to be a bunch of fakes. And they will deliberately denigrate her and the collection and create such controversy that the pieces will be so devalued that it will pay them to wait until she collapses under the burden of disgrace. Then they'll purchase them for pennies. Later they'll say, 'Oops! It looks like the pieces were genuine after all.' We've been down this road before. I'm surprised that you would even suggest such a ploy. No! Find another way."

Believing that this rejection was not sufficiently vehement, he turned to Sensei and said disdainfully, "You can't be serious, Wong. There will be no hammer, fake jar, and *mea culpa*."

"Well," said Sylvia, "I guess that settles it."

"Settles what?" George asked.

"We'll brace ourselves for the bad publicity," she said. "We'll get no coveted invitations. We'll see and hear snickers when we enter a crowded room. But, in time there will be another scandal dancing on foolish tongues, and then it will all be forgotten."

"The suggestion that you publicly smash a copy of the jar is for your protection," Sensei protested, "and that Chinese ginger jar's. You are dealing with drug smugglers. The jar is evidence."

"Evidence of a crime?" Terrell asked angrily. "Evidence of what? You don't know for a fact that any drugs were in that jar. Yes, there's also a little powder in the bottom, but nobody's tested it. We might have two separate things. Talcum powder and the dirty hands of someone in the shipping department." He stood up. "I think we've taken this as far as it can go."

TUESDAY, SEPTEMBER 13, 2011

On the morning news it was announced that the directors of the Museum wanted the public to be reassured that when they visited the museum to see antique Chinese ceramic art, they were seeing the genuine articles. They therefore proposed to sponsor a free seminar on learning how to tell the difference between fake and genuine Chinese ceramics. All interested people should contact the museum - so that the directors would know how large a room they should prepare.

The mood in the Maitlin household had turned hostile. George had asked if anyone minded if he took his coffee up on the roof. No one did and he spent the early morning hours watching the fog roll off the Pacific.

Sensei watched the television coverage of the "Museum's vindication" on the guest room's television. Terrell and Sylvia Maitlin were the subject of a local morning show in which Dr. Gao lamented that there were so many gullible and naive people in the Chinese art market. Dr. Peng revealed the real culprit: the hubris of rich collectors that made them so vulnerable to swindlers and therefore contributed to the degradation of art.

At 9:30 George came back to the guest room minutes before Jake Renquist returned Sensei's call. He lay on his bed as Sensei put the call on speaker.

"After you let me know that Kalahele was on his way back to Honolulu," Jake said, "I put a couple of guys at the terminal. Only one flight was coming in that left Seattle at 4:30, so there was no problem locating him. Just as you said, he came in wearing a Seahawks shirt. He went right to his car and drove to a motel near Diamondhead. He went

36

inside a room and came out with a woman, presumably his wife, who was carrying a kid. My man said the woman looked harried... puffy faced. Then he says, quote, 'Kalahele opened the passenger's side door and the woman got in and bent forward. I couldn't see her face. Kalahele buckled the kid in a car seat in the seat behind her, and then he went back to her and buckled her in. She had her hands over her face, crying.' At least that's what he said it looked like to him. Then Kalahele went around to the driver's side, got in, drove onto the highway and, with one of my men still following him, went home. But get this... my other operative has the sense to see who else was in that motel room. The lights go out, the door opens, and out comes a guy who gets in a car that's registered to a small coffee company that's owned by a local philanthropist named Cheng Lu. Lu is his first name."

"It doesn't take much imagination to see a hostage situation here," Sensei said, "especially when the guy is an art expert and he called a real piece a fake. So tell us more about Cheng Lu."

"He's got a big place in Diamondhead, on Denton Road. Nice real estate. I'm surprised by this. This guy is the 'booster' type. He moves in high society. But my man was thorough. The man who had the wife and kid was a low level employee. There is no way he engineered any complicated art and drugs scheme. I wanted to get your ok before I looked deeper into Cheng Lu. As far as I can tell, this guy flies under the radar. He's got no known association with drugs."

"Neither do the people on this end. They obviously intend to keep it that way. Don't probe this guy unless it looks like we need to go deeper. We're only superficially involved. Fake artwork."

"Nothin's sacred, anymore, Percy. What else can I do for you, hombre?"

Sensei laughed. "Send me a bill."

"Will any guy named William do?" Renquist asked, laughing. It was a joke used to quell the awkwardness of discussing payment.

"Thanks again, Jake. I owe ya'. But I'll still send you two grand for your operatives." Sensei disconnected the call and turned to George. "This whole business is ticking me off. They want us out of here. I got us into this assignment, and I'm feeling responsible for the mess. Look, if the DEA isn't interested and the client doesn't want to make waves, there isn't much more we can do. The morning show coverage has clearly supported the museum's position. Ezra Zhen and the Maitlins are being trashed." Sensei shrugged. "I don't get it. Terrell Maitlin DEA a police commissioner... and yet he seems oblivious to the possibilities of criminal activity."

"He was an insurance salesman," George grinned. "I don't think people who sell insurance ever really believe in disaster. It's always, 'If you should die - God forbid! - you'd want your wife taken care of.' Why should God forbid the inevitable? And the worry isn't that your wife won't be taken care of, it's that you'll croak before you've paid a substantial number of premiums."

Sensei laughed. "Something whacky is goin' on in his mind. But if they don't want to cooperate, we might as well go home. Should we bill him for our time? Or just deduct the airfare?"

George sighed. "Perce, it ain't that simple. This isn't a personal type case... trying to prove a suicide was murder or that John Doe is still alive and well in Peoria. This is serious crime, and if we don't clue up the right people and a cop blunders into it and gets killed, someone's gonna look at us and say, 'You could have prevented this, but all you were worried about was how much you should charge your client for wasting your time.' The Maitlins are honorable people. They'll say that dumping us was their call. But it isn't their call. It's ours. And you've involved Jake Renquist. They've coerced Kalahele. They could kill a cop in Honolulu, too. Up to now people have been regarding this as an art crime. Why not call your 'fatal attraction' in Hong Kong Customs? I know you don't like to call her without a reason, but this is a reason. And maybe the lovely Miss Sonya Lee knows something."

"I was thinking about that, but I didn't want you to get the idea I was trying to mix pleasure with business. Yes, Sonny may know something, or at least she may be able to use her influence to get the DEA to listen to us. I can call her. Don't interrupt me. Give me your phone as backup in case my battery runs down."

"How did you stay single so goddamned long? Wait! What time is it now in Hong Kong?"

"Shit. They're what? Sixteen hours ahead of us. So if it's 10 a.m. Tuesday here, it's 2 a.m. Wednesday there. I can't keep the time zones straight. But I definitely don't want to wake her up."

"Since we have nothing better to do," George suggested, "let's go Christmas shopping and get out of here for a few hours. Then it'll be safe to call her."

"Christmas shopping?"

"Yeah... I'll call my kids and see what they want." As he got out his cellphone, Sensei waved and said he'd go downstairs and look around the house's perimeter for vulnerable areas.

George did not want his children to forget him; but it was getting harder and harder to do anything with them that they could remember. When they were pre-school toddlers, he was hospitalized for gunshot wounds. The shoulder 'brachial plexus' wound and his shattered knee required a year of painful surgeries.

During the early days of his hospitalization, his wife sat and stared at him while he, in a nearly constant morphine haze, remained mostly oblivious to her presence. The number of visits she made to his bedside declined precipitously. Every day. Every other day. Once a week. Stop-ins on her way to an appointment for which she was elegantly dressed. After six months she filed for divorce.

When the divorce was finalized, she told him that her fiancé was rich and unable to have children. He wanted to adopt hers. George refused. She requested no child support, gave him the house and her orchid collection, and moved to California with her new husband and the kids and their dog. When the surgeons had done all they could do for George, he was admitted to a rehab center outside Los Angeles for drug addiction and physical therapy. His wife never brought the children to visit him, and when he would call, she would limit their time on the phone.

When he was fully recovered, the children were old enough to answer the phone themselves. And then, finally, he could talk to them. Beryl got him a laptop with a video connection. Every few months he would fly to California and spend a weekend alone with them. He took them to Disneyland, to the San Diego Zoo, to the beach, to ice skating rinks, and on camping trips.

George was aware that her husband had supported them willingly and had raised them well. He actually admired the man. But as the kids reached their teens, they had social lives of their own. There was little thrill in going anywhere with a parent. He no longer saw them, but he did call regularly to speak to them. He could not text well and the kids rarely looked at email. He would not bother with social media which he considered bubble gum as a substitute for steak. He called them at home and if luck was with him, they'd answer. He had not spoken to his son in six months; and as he lay on the guest room bed, he hoped he'd get lucky.

Someone with a deep voice answered the phone. George asked if George Wagner was there. "It's me, Dad. My voice changed!" George laughed and the two began to discuss prep school and career choices. Finally George asked what he'd like for Christmas. The boy got excited. "I could use another snowboard. We'll be going to Chamonix for Thanksgiving. Chamonix! That's Mont Blanc! A really great board run. My dad got me one of Shaun White's outfits... you know... the 'flying tomato' - white and grey striped pants and jacket. It's really cool." George forced himself to speak pleasantly for another couple of minutes then asked to speak to his daughter. Michelle wanted skis and started to name acceptable and unacceptable brand names. George said he'd try to surprise her. The call ended happily except that George began to tremble. As he would later describe, "I had to slowly draw out the spear that seemed to have sped through the airways and struck me in the chest." His ex-wife's husband was no longer a stepfather. George kept hearing his own son insouciantly refer to him as, "My dad."

When Sensei returned, he took one look at George and knew that the call had been painful. He gave George a half hour to recover and then he tossed him his jacket. "We don't have a car... so we have to beg. If you don't want to go shopping, let's ask Terrell to take us to the museum.

I'd like to see that Japanese ceramic collection. We didn't get to see very much of anything yesterday."

Terrell Maitlin's attitude had worsened. He was being graciously tolerant in a way that seemed to say, "What wonderful guests you are. When will you be leaving?" He thought that it was nice, indeed, that they went to the museum to see one of Seattle's "charms" before they left; but he declined to go with them. Instead he had his driver take them.

They paid their admission fee and headed for the room in which the Japanese ceramics were exhibited; but there was a crowd of people standing in front of the few display cases. "Let's look around and come back later," George said. They moved to the main Chinese section and began to circulate through the aisles of glass-encased exhibits, each with its own card of explanation. They returned to the room that held the Japanese collection and saw that there were still people clustered around the display cases, chattering and ridiculing the pieces with mocking laughter. "Let's pass on the collection," George said. "I'm getting a belly full of baked clay."

They walked back to the administrative offices and were surprised to see Ezra Zhen speaking in a confidential manner with Drs. Gao and Peng and Orville Banning, a member of the museum's board of directors.

The men stopped talking the moment they saw George and Sensei.

George, careful not to overtax his damaged knee, had walked through enough of the aisles. "Let's go back. We can stop for some fast food. I doubt that the Maitlins will put the feed bag on us."

As they turned to leave and started down the stairs, Doctor Peng hurried towards them, calling, "Gentlemen!"

They stopped and looked at him, puzzled. "What is it?" Sensei asked.

"You haven't seen our wonderful Japanese ceramic exhibit. It's on loan from a museum in Kyoto and this is the last day. Since you call yourself 'Sensei' and not 'Sifu,' I thought it might have a special meaning for you. We were just going to inspect the collection. Please... join us. It will be edifying, I'm sure."

George and Sensei looked at each other, shrugged, and still puzzled, climbed the few steps back to join Peng, Orville Banning, and Dr. Sheng

Gao. The five of them went into the room that housed the Japanese collection.

One of the women who had been laughing at the exhibit turned to Dr. Gao and said in a simpering voice that made George cringe, "But these pieces are so crude compared to Chinese porcelain. I should think they'd be ashamed to send them around the world."

"Who can account for fashion?" Banning asked, disparagingly.

"Maybe the potters were going through their Yakuza phase," Dr. Gao quipped and everyone laughed.

"These pieces are childish trash," the woman insisted. "Look at that Oribe tray. The glaze is dripping over the side. In China, the piece would have been discarded. Here, it is considered high art or superb craftsmanship. No... these pieces are neither art nor craft."

"They're not meant to be," Sensei corrected her. "These are essentially sixteenth century Zen pieces. Momoyama Period. Philosophy is driving their style. *Wabi Sabi.*"

"Oh, you mean that quaint business of deliberately making a mistake," she offered.

"No, that is another kind of statement. You'll often find rug makers, for example, deliberately weaving a flaw into the design. The inspiration for the flaw is the spiritual acknowledgement, 'Only God is perfect.' The artist offers up his ego - the praise he would have gotten for having created a perfect rug.

"*Wabi Sabi* is an experience-based interpretation of Buddhism's Four Noble Truths. Craving for more and more things brings us bitterness and pain."

"I've heard the expression '*Wabi Sabi,*'" Banning said, "but I've never been able to figure out what it means." He raised his hands and clapped them. "If anyone's interested - and I know I am - we're going to be given an explanation of *Wabi Sabi*!" Immediately, people within earshot began to come to the Japanese exhibit, forming a semi-circle around Sensei who stood by the glass case.

With two dozen faces eager for an explanation looking at him, the preacher in Sensei rose to the occasion. "Zen distinguishes the eternal from the temporal, or the ethereal - such as Plato's Ideal Forms - from the mundane instances of the form." He pointed to a plain white ceramic spoon from the 16th century. "In the Stone Age people used spoons in exactly the same way that people used them in the 16th century and that we use them today. This function is its natural essence... its eternal significance. But when you add unnatural value to a spoon - for example, use sterling silver spoons - the spoons become more than spoons - they become an egotistic display of wealth. The owner craves people's praise and envy. Veblen called it 'Conspicuous consumption.' That is the opposite of *Wabi Sabi*."

George suddenly felt uneasy. He wondered why directors of a ceramics' museum that was featuring an exhibit of Japanese pottery didn't know what Sensei apparently regarded as fundamental knowledge. This made no sense.

Sensei, assuming that he and George had nothing better to do, continued. "It is absurd to think that in Zen we worship error and poverty and despise perfection and wealth. We eliminate excess to apprehend purity. We strive not to need anything that exceeds the need to function well in a natural capacity or environment. A spoon may be old and worn, but if it does its job, it holds its own and keeps its place of honor among spoons.

"The natural essence of a spoon remains apart from its substance or fashion. Form follows function. The reason that Mies Van der Rohe's dictum, 'Less is more,' continues to have meaning is that it is easier to recognize purity when it is shorn of decorative excess. Zen, therefore, stresses the beauty of 'elegant simplicity.' There is nothing baroque in Zen design."

George burst into the discussion. "There you have it! And right from the horse's mouth." He tugged at Sensei's sleeve.

"But just a bit more," Dr. Peng insisted. "Please. At least tell us why a man must be a hermit to appreciate this *Wabi Sabi*."

Sensei felt that it was important to answer. That was his job, explaining the Dharma. George, he was certain, was still upset about the phone call. He continued, "What is difficult to understand about Zen's concept of 'Wabi Sabi' is solitude. There is a difference between loneliness and solitude. Loneliness is anguish. Solitude is contentment. But just being glad to be alone is not *Wabi Sabi*. To live apart from others because they reject us, or because we reject them, is not *Wabi Sabi*. That is negative. *Wabi Sabi* is positive. We embrace solitude in a transcendental state which, by definition, means that we are not burdened with ego. In the spiritual world there is stillness, an unconditional peace in which we seek nothing more than to harmonize with the natural order of our surroundings."

"But what has this to do with sloppy glazing?" the woman asked.

"Sloppy is an ego-judgment. When we are in the meditative level of kenosis, a state of consciousness in which the ego is absent, the world becomes exquisite in its pristine splendor... exactly as it is.

"The dripping of the glaze on the tray was not done deliberately, as if the artist wished to say that there is beauty in error. That would be contrived... ego-conscious. Rather, the artist had transcended the temporal and material world, and his Buddha Self, Amitabha, or God, if you prefer, was therefore in control of the process. The artist, by definition, was absent, and it was the hands of God that were making the tray. God does not produce people or things with cookie-cutter sameness. Consider snowflakes! When the artist is lost in the splendor of the egoless world his brush may dip too deeply into the glaze. The dripping glaze is neither admired nor despised."

Banning was smarmy in his response. "But how can you tell whether the mistake is deliberate, accidental, or the result of divine intervention?"

"You can't. But that's *your* problem. When an artist enters that egoless zone he is no longer enslaved by desires to be praised or by fears of being mocked. He's beyond the need to conform, and how you value his work is irrelevant.

"You can study the principles of *Wabi Sabi* but you won't understand them until you've attained *Satori*, the extinguishing of ego or 'small mind.' Elegant simplicity. It can be old, crude, unpolished, or a little beat up." He pointed to a bowl. "That Raku tea bowl... the black one. If it is an original it must be worth many thousands of dollars because it is old and rare. Actually it is priceless. How can you purchase the vision of a saint?"

Orville Banning gushed at the beauty of Sensei's explanation. "How clear you've made it! But tell us," he begged, "what of this other red bowl?"

George raised a hand and then took Sensei by the sleeve. In a firm voice he announced, "We've got another appointment to keep. Sorry folks."

As they descended the stairs, Sensei asked, "What appointment?"

"There's no appointment. I just started to get creeped out by this sudden interest in Zen philosophy. It was like we were being stalled or something."

It was after two o'clock when Charles, the driver, stopped to let them out at the portico and continued on to park in the rear of the house. Before he could ring the doorbell, Sensei noticed that the door was not completely shut. "Look at this," he said.

"I'm not carrying, Perce... so you better be prepared for a little hand to hand."

Sensei pushed the door open. Commissioner Maitlin was bound and gagged, lying across the threshold of the gallery-living room. Sensei tore the tape from his mouth. "Where's your wife?"

"Upstairs."

George bounded up the stairs and found Sylvia Maitlin swollen-eyed, bound and gagged. Her hands were cuffed behind her with what George called, "a first edition zip tie." The door to Sylvia's closet was open and he could see several leather belts hanging on a hook. He grabbed one and inserted the buckle's prong into the lock to reverse the locking pin. "Ease your hands out," he said, as he widened the constricting loops.

Sylvia rubbed her wrists and began to whimper, "They wanted my jar. They went right to where I usually keep it—"

"Terrell's ok. Is anyone in the house except your husband?"

"Ok? Was he hurt?"

"He's fine! Is anyone else in the house?"

"No. It's the maid's day off and the cook went out with the houseboy to buy something special for dinner, and Charles was with you."

Sylvia was still unsteady on her feet. George had to help her descend the stairs. She saw the open gallery door and gasped.

"You're lucky someone else wasn't hurt." George, having little tolerance for people who refused to listen to reason, tried not to sound harsh, but he was still chafing from the "My dad" comment his son had made.

Sylvia was not listening. Her attention was fixed on the cabinets of porcelain; and before going to see how her husband was, she ran to a closet and opened its door. She sank to her knees, opened the box, and sighed with relief. "It's still here!"

George continued to grouse. "Some day explain to me why people call in a professional to get his advice and then refuse to take it." Sensei nudged him, indicating that he should soften his tone.

Terrell Maitlin was embarrassed by his wife's lack of attention to him. "I'm glad you're not harmed, dear," he said in an accusing tone.

"Now that we've got our priorities established," George said sarcastically, "maybe we can talk some sense into you."

Terrell Maitlin rubbed his wrists. "What do you want us to do? You'll get no further arguments from me."

Sensei looked at George and began to speak to the Maitlins. "First, you have to understand that if your cook and maid had been at home and had tried to save you they'd probably be lying dead in the kitchen. You not only placed your own lives at risk, but you put other people's lives at risk as well. Your reputations as 'porcelain experts' are not worth the kind of heartache you can cause yourself and others."

Sylvia helped her husband into a chair and then proceeded to sit on the floor at his feet. "I was terrified," she said, whining.

"That's how people generally respond when their lives are threatened," George said. "You will very likely be attacked again."

"What makes you think there's going to be another attack?" Terrell countered, forgetting his assurance that he would no longer be argumentative.

George's mood had not changed. Gruffly, he said, "They didn't get what they came for. Let's go over again exactly what happened when you were attacked."

Sylvia reached up, but her husband declined to hold her hand. Terrell related, "Sylvia was upstairs. The servants were out. There was a knock at the door. I opened it. There was a girl in dark glasses standing outside. She attacked me. She punched, pushed, and kicked me hard... and then a man jumped into the room. He wore dark clothing, like one of those ninja people you see on television. He tossed me face down and bound my hands while the girl put tape on my mouth. Then they went right upstairs to Sylvia. I heard her scream but I couldn't do anything. They bound my ankles, too."

Sylvia picked up the narrative. "The two of them burst into our bedroom and went right to where I usually keep the box. But I had put it down here... in the closet. I'm going to take it to get a teakwood stand for it. I don't care what people say about my beautiful porcelain jar."

"Will you shut up about that goddamned jar!" Maitlin snapped. He let his fingers indicate a half-inch. "I am this far away from smashing it, myself!"

George held up a hand. "What happened upstairs?"

Sylvia pouted. "He demanded I tell him where the box was. He had a Chinese accent. I told him Doctor Gao called and asked me to bring the jar to the museum. I said that Gao told me that he had a teakwood stand for it and he wanted to give it to me as a peace offering. The two of them did not like that news. I could tell they felt double-crossed or something. He grabbed me by the hair and flung me down onto the floor and they bound me. He told me I was lying and that he was going to kill me if I didn't tell him where the jar was. I kept insisting that I had given it to Dr. Gao for him to measure and fit a teakwood base on." She softened her tone. "We were wrong not to listen. I was wrong in putting my reputation before the safety of the members of my household. Ah!" she exclaimed. "Max! Where is Max?"

The driver had parked the car and entered the house through a side door.

"Charles!" Terrell shouted. "Have you seen Max? Go out back and see if you can find him."

Nobody said anything as the driver's footsteps went to the back door, opened and closed it. A moment later, Charles burst into the kitchen. "He's dead out here! Oh, there's blood all over! It looks like his throat's been cut!"

"Are you sure he's dead?" Terrell Maitlin stood up as his wife swung her legs around to let him pass.

Charles stood in the steel doorway. "He's dead! His head has practically been cut off."

George said nothing. He knew that anyone can make a mistake; but the Maitlins had not erred. They acted in accordance with their own reasoned deliberations. They were foolish people and George did not suffer fools gladly. He got up and went outside to sit on the portico steps. He wanted to be alone where he could flush old thoughts out of his mind. He kept remembering his old dog... that went west with the kids. And now Max was dead. He felt that same old keen and helpless disappointment. He got up and went back into the house.

Sensei had used the time to explain that a professional likes his clients to be more receptive to suggestions. Terrell and Sylvia Maitlin now understood. They smiled as George approached.

"I don't think I want anything more to do with you people," George said simply. "I'll get my things from the bedroom." He turned to Sensei. "See that they notify the police. And tell them how those sons of bitches at the museum tried to stall us from getting back here."

Sensei followed him to the staircase. "I know they were trying to stall us. I got carried away. Look, we're here now," he said. "Give these folks another chance."

"What's that line? Give them a second chance to make the same mistake again? No, you handle it with Sonya, maybe she can make the DEA listen. But they have to report this home-invasion to the police."

"Then wait until I call her. If she thinks there's a problem here, stay with me and help me to solve it. I can't do it without you. Don't make me look like a fool in front of Sonya."

George seemed not to care that his clients were in hearing distance. "I'm not in the mood to take any more shit from those idiots."

Sylvia burst out crying. "I know it's our fault... my fault. I know I should have listened." She called to George, "Don't go. Please give us another chance."

"We're here," Sensei said. "Let's finish the job. I'll warn them that the next time they give us an argument, we're through. Ok? Let's go back in."

George lectured himself about being professional. "All right. Go call Sonya." Grudgingly he returned to the gallery-living room.

George looked at Terrell and Sylvia. "Send Charles down to the Animal Control center immediately and have him adopt a terrier-size dog. Tell him to make sure it's house broken. Tell him to take a leash with him and to walk with the dog before he pays the fee. Any 'ready to go' small mutt will do. Male or female." He was tempted to say something sarcastic, but he checked himself.

He waited for Terrell to call Charles, but Terrell just sat there looking at George as if he were wondering what George was doing in his home.

George shouted, "Wake up! Call Charles in here!"

"I'm sorry," Terrell whined, "I'm willing to do whatever you want me to do. I didn't understand what you were asking. My wife was almost killed. And Max. He was a good dog. Tell me again what you want. Two terriers?"

George sat down and summoned patience. "Terrier-size! A small dog. Little dogs are the best house protectors. They bark defensively. And they don't investigate what they bark at. Little dogs tend to be so nervous that they react before anyone has the time to bribe them with pork chops. So for your wife's protection you need a dog that will alert to any person setting foot in or around the house. It may be noisy... but don't get into the 'cry wolf' state of mind. When the dog barks, arm yourself and go see what the problem is. A human guard won't be able to give you such an early warning. Humans think. And a thinking employee is usually smart enough to protect himself and look out for number one - and that isn't you. So far, do you understand?"

Terrell and Sylvia nodded but they still made no move to carry out George's first directive.

Charles had been listening in the doorway. "Perhaps Mr. and Mrs. Maitlin may be in shock. Give them a minute."

George was not in the mood to be sympathetic, but he softly repeated, "Tell Charles to go to the dog pound!"

"Charles," Sylvia said, "Would you go now and get a 'ready-to-go' small dog for us. Take it for a walk to be sure it's... well... civilized."

George continued. "Do you have weapons in the house and can you use them?"

They had one gun. Sylvia had fired a rifle, but never a handgun. George asked Terrell, "Do you have one of those smart phones?"

"Yes."

"Look up the nearest gun shop and ask them if your wife buys a hand gun... will they teach her how to use it. You'll pay extra for the lessons. If they say yes, tell them your wife will be there as soon as possible to buy a weapon. She can pick one that fits best in her hand... and have her first lesson. She can take lessons during the waiting period. Do you have another car for her to use?"

"Yes," Sylvia said. "I have my own car. But... a gun?" She looked at George. "A gun is fine! I've always wanted a good gun."

Terrell Maitlin had reached a gun shop. He asked about the handgun and the lessons. "Her name is Sylvia Maitlin. I'm former police commissioner Terrell Maitlin. At 3 p.m.?" He looked down at Sylvia who nodded in agreement. "She'll be there." He looked at his wife. "You may have to wait to get the gun until the feds check you out... but you can go there every day to get lessons and practice."

George continued. "Get it through your heads that you have disrupted a drug smuggling operation. There is not the slightest doubt in my mind that your jar was once filled with heroin. And they no doubt think that you somehow screwed up their operation. Try to understand! The people at the museum who fouled up are going to have to shift the blame onto someone, and that someone is likely to be you. One way or another, they'll finger you. You don't even know if it was they or a rival gang of traffickers that attacked you. You have no idea about the kind of danger you're in. And don't think you can just leave town until everything blows over. They know where your kids live. They'd slit their own family's throats for a kilo of heroin.

"Only a few individuals would have access to a genuine imperial piece of ceramics. You, by your own insistence on the jar's authenticity, have exposed them to criminal investigation and made them targets. They may have had nothing to do with the drug operation, but you've put the spotlight on them. Where did that piece come from so that heroin could have been put into it before it was packed for shipment? You don't know. Anti-drug agencies will make it their business to find out. Meanwhile, the shipper of those drugs will want to know what damage you've done to them with your reports to the DEA and so on. And if they decide to find out, you've got a serious problem. The shippers are probably hoping that you have the good sense to play along with the fake jar ploy. End the controversy about the jar. Get on the phone and call the most agreeable local TV news program you know and schedule a hammer smashing 'mea culpa' session. Do you own a reasonably similar jar now?"

Sylvia spoke mechanically. "My cook uses ones that resembles it."

"Fine. Go and smash it in front of the cameras and say, 'So much for fake art. I've learned my lesson.' Try to sound as if you mean it. Think of Max and get mad. The crooks will lament that you're so stupid that you'd smash an authentic jar; but it may make them decide to scratch you off the list of people who are out to hurt them. Do you understand?"

Instantly Sylvia Maitlin was on her feet making her way to the kitchen. In a moment she returned with a cheap storage jar of the same approximate shape, color, and decoration as the valuable original. Terrell Maitlin owed the manager of the most widely watched local news program a favor so he decided to give him the scoop. Sylvia would be at the TV station at 9 a.m. the next morning.

George continued, "Break the jar in a cardboard box and bring all of the pieces home with you. Leave nothing there for anyone to examine. But right now I want Sylvia to go to her gun lesson. Get a semi-automatic. Nothing too big for you to handle. Mr. Maitlin can question the servants while you're gone. We need to know whether or not they noticed anyone lurking around the house... any cars... any phone calls.

"Mrs. Maitlin can try to recall how many people knew that she kept the box in the bedroom. The servants knew. Did Ezra know?"

"Yes," Sylvia said. "He came here when I called to tell him how the dog alerted. I told him that I had to keep the jar in our bedroom to keep it safe."

"We have to regard him as being involved," George said. "He may be perfectly innocent, but we can't take that chance.

"And today the three museum administrators tried to engage Percy in long-winded explanations of Japanese pottery. Percy's knowledge of Japanese ceramics is cursory. They are the experts who ought to be explaining basic concepts to us. I believe that they knew that this house was going to be searched for that jar and they wanted to give your assailants time to complete the job. This situation is much worse that we previously believed.

"Now… you have two choices. Your life in this house is not likely to be happy and comfortable. You've been invaded and while you may not feel the full impact of that now, you will soon. If they want you, you won't be able to hide. So you've got to realize that this is a kind of war and you've got to get into a combat mode. We can help. The moment we get far enough into the problem to identify it, the federal and state authorities will take over. It would probably be best if you let your servants go on vacation. The reality is that if they held a knife to your cook's throat, you would hardly decline to cooperate with them. Think it over."

"Why would they want to force us to do anything? We don't know anything," Terrell said.

George sighed in frustration. "They don't know that. You've involved yourselves in a crime; and somebody has fouled up by letting that jar get out of the museum. A guilty person would implicate you in order to divert suspicion from himself."

Terrell and Sylvia looked at each other. Sylvia whispered, "Terrell, pull yourself together. If it's war, we'll fight. I guess the gun shop owner will let me try on a bunch of guns to see which one of them fits me."

George checked his watch. It's two thirty," he said to Sylvia. "Don't be late for school."

As Sylvia left the room, George said, "It's time we looked at your gun." Terrell led George back to his den and removed a Smith and Wesson .38 revolver from a drawer in a side table. "If you don't have cleaning and oiling supplies on hand, order them when you call the gun shop with your order for a box of .38 rounds."

Sonya Lee saw Sensei's caller I.D. and answered, "I'm sorry. I accept calls only from handsome men named Percy." And then she disconnected the call. A moment later her phone rang again and, as expected, Sensei could not stop laughing. Finally he said, "Did I wake you up?" And she answered, "No, my Valkyrie ring tone did." Again he laughed. "All right, Brynhilde, I need your help." "Of course you do," she said and again he giggled.

Sonya was already familiar with the case. "I've known about the fake imperial jar and the dog alerting to it for a couple of weeks," she said. "My boss sent a memo about it to the art forgery section of criminal investigations. The drugs' involvement is incidental to the art fraud."

"Sonya, I think you've got it backwards. I think this jar - and by the way, this is no pint sized jar... George said it could hold ten pounds of coffee beans when he first saw it - this ginger jar was used to smuggle heroin into the U.S. The dog alerted to it. Consider how the jar was shipped. It was put into a thin plastic bag and encased in a kind of ballistics gel... almost a square meter of it. Then the square was encased in styrofoam inside a wooden crate. Customs can look through the gel and see that it is an antique jar... nobody goes to that length to protect a fake jar when shipping it. So the jar is special. The shipper is a reputable shipper... maybe even a government agency. The consignee is an established museum with perhaps municipal or state government connections. What is Customs going to do? Melt the gel? Then repackage the piece and let it continue on its way?

"No... this is not an art fraud case. This is a drug smuggling case that involves a piece of ceramic art."

There was a long silence on the phone. "Sonya?" Sensei called.

"Quiet! I'm thinking!"

He waited until she was ready to speak.

"Percy, this makes more sense to me than you can possibly imagine. I've always had these loose ends sticking out of certain cases... and I've never been able to tie them up. Are you going to be in Seattle for long?"

"If you need me here, I'll be here. But you have to tell me what you want. I have a temple and karate students... you know my responsibilities.

Although I have people covering for me, I don't want to abuse their kindness. But solving this case is important. A few hours ago they broke---"

"---Na na na na.... Don't tell me anything over this line. Go get yourself a burner phone and call me back. I've got a new prepaid cell here that I can use. When you call back, I'll give you the number. Do you remember that code we worked out in San Diego? We were kidding around, but I'm sure you remember it. Are we clear on this? After you get your prepaid phone, you call me on your regular phone and I'll give you my prepaid cell number in code and you'll give me yours in code."

"Yes, my love. Perfectly clear," he said.

"And... did I tell you how much I miss you?"

"No, you didn't."

"Good, I hate to have to lie. Ciao." She disconnected the call.

"She loves me!" he said aloud and went to ask someone to take him to a phone shop.

At dinner Sylvia's personality had changed. "I hate to say it, but with a Beretta in my hand, I felt a sense of power. I'd like to keep one in every room. I mean... why not? We don't have children in the house."

"Now, dear," Terrell said. "Let's not get carried away."

"Don't you mean... 'Let's not get carried away in a body bag'? At the very least I'm going to wear western clothing and either get a shoulder holster or wear a gun belt. And a Kevlar vest that looks western. And as soon as I can hit what I'm aiming at, I'm going to apply for a concealed weapon permit."

Sensei cleared his throat. "We've got a customs agent coming from Hong Kong." He placed a small tape recorder on the table in front of her dinner plate. "Tell me anything and everything that comes into your mind about that dealer in Singapore, the people at the museum, and with Ezra Zhen. The agent's name is Sonya Lee."

"One. I have never dealt with Smith-Cheung Antiques - the dealer in Singapore. From what I've heard, they buy and sell with galleries, art auction houses, museums, commercial outlets like Ezra Zhen's shop, and large private collectors. Ezra told me their office is on the 48th floor of a building. Not exactly foot traffic. So they're what you'd call 'wholesale' as opposed to 'retail.'

"Two. While I did tell Ezra that I'd be by to see the jar he told me about, I didn't specify the time. When I got there I asked him if I could go back and watch the melting process. So, while I didn't have an appointment, he would probably have guessed that I'd be there as soon as possible.

"Three. Because Ezra Zhen is in that coveted circle, he has connections both to the dealer and the museum. Museums buy and sell the items they display. They usually have twice as many articles in back rooms than they have out front on display. So that he would buy something from them is not unusual. I saw the gel drip off the piece. I feel confident that he didn't receive any drugs in the jar. Also, if he were involved in the drug traffic, I can't imagine why he wouldn't have told them not to offer the jar for sale or returned it when he discovered what it was. But whether the museum took the drugs out and repacked the jar or whether they never opened it at all, I don't know."

Sylvia Maitlin stood up and walked away from the table. "I went out and looked at Max. We're supposed to call the dead animal disposal people but I decided that he died in the line of duty and deserved a proper resting place. I asked Charles to dig a grave. At sundown, Terrell and I and the servants will have a little service. How could anybody be so cruel? If only I had listened."

"Let's just get the guys who did it," George said.

Sensei gave her the digital recorder. "Keep this with you and record everything you remember about the names on the crate, or comments you heard regarding the controversy. And include the names of people you've spoken to about the jar - at the museum, Ezra's shop... anywhere."

She picked up the recorder. "I'm going into the living room... when I'm around my collection I remember more details about each piece. First I'll get my daybook. That has all my notes in it. I hope they didn't take my daybook."

WEDNESDAY, SEPTEMBER 14, 2011

Everyone watched Sylvia's performance on the morning show. She had sprayed the jar with glossy polyurethane to make it shine and reflect so much light that no one could get a good look it. On top of the glossy coating, she sprayed light cooking oil on it. Watching at home, George and Sensei could see only a flashing blue and white jar. "She's amazing," George said.

As if she were giving a cooking lesson, she had held the jar out for inspection before placing it in a cardboard box. Then she took the hammer she brought from her hobby room and began whacking the jar, keeping in cadence the blow and each stressed syllable of her iambic pentameter utterance, "This is - the way - to purge - the world - of fakes." The camera peeked inside the box at several intervals. She explained in a few short but pithy sentences the inestimable damage fakes cause in the art world.

George pronounced her performance, "extremely convincing." In the interview after, Terrell Maitlin reminded everyone of his wife's courage in destroying something beautiful for the integrity of future purchases of Chinese porcelains. Terrell picked up the box that contained, as he put it, "the shards of shame" and carried it out of the studio.

They had gone to the studio in separate cars. Terrell put the box in the trunk of his car and returned home. Sylvia went to the gun shop. She had scheduled one morning and one afternoon lesson. Terrell would join her for the afternoon session. In the previous day's lesson, she had been able to hit the paper target only twice. Her score was 2-28. In her second, she hit the target paper four times for a score of 4-26. "I'm getting the hang of this," she announced to her instructor. He replied, "You'll be a regular Annie Oakley." The reference encouraged her and she stopped at a western clothing and boot shop and bought herself an outfit to go with her new gun belt. The clerk did not know how to answer her when she asked if she could put a Beretta Px4 Storm in the revolver's holster.

At home, eating lunch, she revealed her improvement and announced that she was going to try to shoot with her left hand, as well. "I've always held my fork in my left hand when I eat. And I've played the piano. It ought not be too great a feat." George and Sensei and Terrell looked at each other and nodded in her direction. "Yes..." George concurred. "A real feat."

Sensei asked Terrell to rent two cars. As long as they were going to be involved with an investigation that included Sonya Lee and other agents in China, he needed to be independently mobile. George, too, needed to be independently mobile and with Sylvia taking lessons so often, he could not depend on her for transportation.

As Terrell and Sylvia left to take their afternoon shooting lesson, George and Sensei accompanied them and were dropped off at the car rental place. They each rented a four-wheel drive SUV.

With an envelope containing ten glossy Qing jar photographs tucked under her arm, Beryl saluted the bronze statue of Rocky Balboa and began the long walk to the cascading steps of the Art Museum. She entered the majestic building, told the receptionist that she had an appointment with Douglas Carville, and waited until the receptionist called him and received his permission to let her pass.

Carville's office was at the far end of the North Wing and she, in effect, retraced her steps. She was wearing high-heeled shoes and between the long walk to and up the steps and the walk back to Carville's office in the huge museum, she had clocked, she thought, at least a mile. Doug was waiting for her at his office door. "Bonjour, Madame," he said smiling.

"My dogs are barking," she replied and playfully shoved him into his office so that she could take her shoes off. "Here," she said, thrusting the envelope at him. "Please tell me that Dr. Dao Wu is next door. If it's any farther, I'll need an ambulance."

"Relax, he's on his way over." Before she could check to see if blisters had formed on her heels, Doctor Dao Wu opened Carville's office door.

The Chinese scholar, tall, wide eyed, and of an African and Chinese racial mix, entered and slid his palms into his jacket sleeves in the manner of a oriental magistrate. "Confucius say," Wu had to imitate a Chinese accent since he had none of his own, "man who fly upside down..." Everyone laughed at the old joke.

Carville handed him the photographs. Wu's smile turned to an open-mouthed awe. "Fantastic!" he exclaimed. "Guan Yao! The Imperial kiln. Nian Hao! All the dates and I.D. are here and they're perfectly written." He needed only a glance at the Imperial seal marks. Wu had been born and raised in Hong Kong and the writing was as familiar to him as his own rendition of the characters. "This is a piece made for the Guangxu Emperor Zaitian, known posthumously as Jingdi. There is absolutely no doubt about this. I'd have had more trouble reading it if it were inscribed in Mao ordained new script. And I like that it's been photographed while someone is holding it. It gives a better sense of the size.

"Jingdi reigned from 1875 to 1908. Look at the condition of this piece! It's mint! Perfect. The wide mouth suggests that it was made for hands that reached into it... an arm that could have reached to the bottom. Since this piece did not store foodstuff as would be used in the kitchen, it was likely kept in the dining room. Perhaps the Emperor had it filled with candy or with little favors. Just as you get a fortune cookie and take delight in opening it and reading, 'Help! I am being held prisoner in a Chinese bakery!' or some other edifying news, the party-animals at court could have reached in to get their wisdom-fix for the day. And then they'd giggle and exchange the intel.

"Sometimes the Emperor would order the jar to be filled with water and a lily with a small lily pad would float on the surface and there would be a few little goldfish in there that would come to the surface for crumbs that the Emperor tossed on the water. In the North where it is bloody cold in the winter, the sight of a blooming lotus flower was better than Valium. Beautiful. Doug said it was consigned to a museum in Seattle. Who was the shipper?"

"Smith-Cheung of Singapore. They don't know to whom, specifically, in the museum it was consigned."

"They're legit. So what's the problem with this piece?"

Beryl asked, "Do you know Herbert Kalahele?"

"Sure. Good man."

"On Monday he looked at the piece and said that the characters for *Guang* and *Zhi* were written in modern script. They lacked the proper number of strokes. He pronounced the jar a fake."

"Herb said that? He must have been joking… or else somebody held a gun to his head. These characters are precisely what they're supposed to be."

"Mrs. Maitlin, the owner, was angry when he made his determination. There had been a thin rubber collar on the jar's neck that he removed when he examined the piece. She said that she had neglected to put the collar on when she put the jar in its box and the lid scraped the rim and Kalahele snapped at her, 'Be careful!' She's convinced he knew it was genuine. We have other evidence, too, that his family was threatened, held hostage in Honolulu. We've got good reason to suspect that heroin was smuggled into the country inside this jar. Hong Kong Customs is looking into it. It would be prudent if you didn't discuss the jar or anything about the jar. This meeting didn't take place. Until we know what we're dealing with, an association with the jar could be risky."

"Hong Kong Customs? Do you have the name of any specific agent? I know a few of them."

"Miss Sonya Lee."

Doctor Dao Wu reached into his pocket and produced a business card. "Please give Sonny my card… just in case she lost the last two that I gave her. Who knows? Maybe she forgot me. Tell her I am at her service. Whatever she wants me to do, I'll do. And I'm not limiting that to porcelain… like her complexion."

Doug Carville laughed. "Is there something I ought to know?"

Beryl grinned. "Nothing except she's very beautiful and is a Gung Fu expert. But to return to the jar, I have a question. Where do you think it's been all these years?"

"It could have been held in a warehouse or some storage facility. If it had been in a museum we'd know about it. Since its condition is so perfect I doubt that it was exposed to a household's normal wear and tear. Yes, it could have been in someone's home - if the person didn't have kids and did have very careful servants. There were so few of these big jars made. They presented a higher degree of difficulty - shaping them symmetrically, firing them, spacing the painted designs properly, shipping them overland by cart to a destination that could be a thousand miles away. Usually, for an unusual piece of this sort, they'd have to deliver three perfect specimens. It's like traveling in the rough. You take three changes of clothing: one you're wearing; one's being laundered; and one's clean, waiting in the backpack or drawer. The court could dine with the Emperor and eat from many royal dishes, but there would be only one of these jars for the royal dining room. If it broke, they'd have a replacement. But they probably wouldn't order more jars until the second jar broke. The Emperor reigned thirty-three years. He died without an heir. I doubt that he needed many of these jars." Wu stopped speaking and looked sheepishly at Beryl and Doug. "But I don't seem to be answering your question. All right. I'll make an effort to stay on topic.

"For what it's worth, this is gossip. You've probably never heard of the Mong Tai heroin connection in Myanmar. Khun Sa of eastern Burma is the Da Wong - the big king - of the trafficking operation. I once heard a colleague remark that he moved so much heroin through Thailand that he ought to be called 'The King of Siam.' This monarch of the drug trade and an assortment of friends and relatives have palaces somewhere in that Golden Triangle... domiciles that are stuffed with valuable Chinese porcelains. I'm told that one of his group had an affair with a blonde archeologist who lives in Santa Fe, New Mexico. His wife hated all the Chinese 'knick knacks' and wanted the joint refurbished in Danish Modern. If he wanted to send his girlfriend something valuable, shipping her some of these artworks would be one way to beat the money-transfer watchers. She could tell the IRS it was worth $2000 and how could they argue? Nobody knows the true value of these pieces anymore. The Chinese have destroyed their own market by flooding it with fakes. This is just a wild guess. I'm trying to connect the dots... heroin... smuggling... antique jars... Singapore shipper. I'm also considering the market demand for a fake and the cost of making a fake. It's like counterfeiting a ten thousand dollar bill. You can make a great copy, but who wants to handle it? There just isn't a big demand for big jars. But how this jar got from a museum to a flagrantly incorrect appraisal, I can't help you there."

Now that George had resumed a professional attitude toward the case, he began to consider the gel-melting procedure that Ezra Zhen had followed and also the significant but offhand comment Zhen made to Sylvia about the gelatin's reusability. If the museum had unpacked the jar and then resealed it in gelatin, identifiable bits of debris - trace evidence - could easily have fallen into the gel. He would need the gel and, he reasoned, samples of dirt removed by dustpan and by vacuum cleaner in whichever room in the museum that the gel had been liquified.

At dinner, George questioned Sylvia. "You said that Ezra collected the gelatin. I'm assuming that the big plastic bag he had in the tub is the same bag it was shipped in. Do you know if he kept that bag, and if so, where it is now?"

"The last I saw it," Sylvia replied, "it was sitting on the floor beside a cabinet, against a wall in his work room. The top was knotted so that the gel wouldn't spill out. It was there as of a week ago," she said.

"Why are you interested in the gelatin?" Terrell Maitlin asked.

George prepared himself for another bout of Maitlin resistance. "If the jar was unpacked in the museum, bits of debris specific to the museum may have fallen into the gel. If we can find and then identify them, it may prove that the drugs were received there."

"Oh," Sylvia gasped, "just like trace evidence! I know a way to enter the museum through the sewer!"

Terrell Maitlin slapped his knees. "That is out of the question!"

"You're right," George replied. "No need to do anything stupid. We can get what we need from trash bins left outside. Dust pan sweepings and vacuum cleaner bags should be enough."

"Uh, oh!" Sylvia warned. "I would not trust any forensic people in this area to look for trace evidence. You know what I think? I think we should get the whole bag of gel and as many museum dirt deposits as we can, and we should ship both containers of them to your friend in Honolulu. Sensei told me that his contact in Honolulu had good police resources. We can pay anything they want."

Maitlin scoffed. "And you propose to go dumpster diving for museum dirt and perhaps break into Ezra Zhen's shop with its well-wired security system? And you don't think you'll be caught? How will you feel when a security camera's photograph of you rummaging in a dumpster or picking a lock is published? Think about what you're suggesting."

"What's there to think about?" Sylvia countered. "This is the best damned lead we've had. I think we should get the dirt as soon as possible. The longer we wait, the more the dirt's character can change. Should I put on a dumpster diving *ensemble* right now?"

"No," Terrell said. "Let's get more information about this... this dirt quest."

"Don't worry," George tried to mollify his host. "I won't let her do anything dangerous or illegal."

"I'm glad to hear that you'll be taking such good care of my wife. I suppose you won't be needing me to come along on your treasure hunt. What, specifically, do you hope to find?"

"I wish you would come. The museum isn't a restaurant. The dirt in the bins is likely to be dry and free of flies and such. The best debris will be from living organisms... say, a cat. I don't know if the museum has a cat - many do because of the damage mice can do - and if a cat's hair or a human hair - with a follicle preferably - is present in the gel and has a DNA match to a cat or person in the museum, we've got positive proof that the jar was unpacked there and then repacked for Ezra to open. Cat and human hair can be swept up or vacuumed easily. It's not the time of year for pollen - but that is one source of organic material that could identify a place.

"And we'll have to stop at a drug store and get a box of latex gloves. Sensei and I can get into Zhen's place and take the gel. We'll go when he's turned off the system. Mrs. Maitlin can distract him. It isn't as though we'd be stealing anything that would rise above misdemeanor value."

Sensei stood up. "Come on, Boss," he said to Maitlin. "We'll make an adventure of it."

Sylvia ran upstairs to change her clothes. When she re-appeared, she was dressed in denim and had a tool belt on. "I'm ready for anything," she said. "Flashlight. Hammer. Pliers. Cellphone. You name it. I've got it."

The museum's exhibition rooms were dark, but lights were on in the administrative offices and the repair and storage rooms in the rear of the building.

"What can they be doing this late?" Sylvia wondered aloud.

"Maybe they're planning their course in Fake Porcelain Detection," Sensei joked.

Terrell Maitlin parked in the rear beside a room that had been added-on to the otherwise square building. George wondered what the room's function was, but before he had a chance to inquire, Sylvia immediately jumped out of the car and ran to the dumpster. As she lifted its lid, she called, "I've hit the mother lode! Two whole vacuum cleaner bags... filled." She also removed several trashcan liner-bags that the cleaning people used when they went from office to office, emptying trashcans into their cleaning cart. She handed George the bags and vaulted out of the dumpster. "When do you want to hit Zhen's?" she asked, as Maitlin pulled away.

"At any time that you can talk him out of the building. How about if you drive there in the morning and Sensei and I will follow. You can let the air out of a tire and go into the shop to ask him to help you change the tire. When you go in to ask him, if it is possible for you to unlock the back door, we'll go in and get the bag and get back out again. Does his back door also have a sliding bolt?"

"No... just a dead bolt."

"Too bad," George exclaimed. "The job just got harder."

"No," she said, "easier. The shop is a corner property. I know where he keeps his keys... even a spare one that I can leave for you. I'll pretend to need to wash my hands and I'll unlock the dead bolt and put the key outside on a fence post. You can park on the side street. We won't be able to see you, and then you can just let yourself in and out. Lock the door again on your way out. You may have to jump the fence."

"Can we locate a copy of the sales' receipt for the jar?" George asked.

"He doesn't use a computer, so there's nothing you can hack into. He doesn't have what you'd call a large volume of sales. I'd say that if he buys and sells one piece a week, he's ahead of the game. He carries only expensive pieces."

"Did you ever see him make an entry? Does he write in Chinese or English?"

"English. But sometimes he makes a note in Chinese characters. And he writes out a sales slip on one of those pre-loaded metal tablet things that's got a carbon paper feed. There's an original white slip, and then a yellow copy and a pink copy. He gives the customer the white original. A number is pre-printed on the bottom of all three copies. He writes in Chinese characters sometimes when he fills out a gift card. The spare key is under the ink and brush tray."

"Is there an easy way to see August's receipts?"

"To my knowledge he keeps his sales tickets on a spindle on his desk. He keeps the various receipts for stuff he buys, clipped together, right beside it. His accountant picks them up, so I don't know if they'll be there."

The servants had not wanted to take any more time off. They had returned after one day and were now retired for the evening.

Sylvia made a pot of coffee and she, Terrell, George, and Sensei sat at the kitchen table to discuss the case. Sensei wanted the Maitlins to be involved in any monetary discussions. He called Jake Renquist and explained the gel and dirt analysis, then he put the call on speakerphone and told the unnamed clients that they were free to ask any questions. "Can you get people to do it?" Sensei asked.

"Getting the gel and the trash examined comes down to money. There's no way to estimate the time it will take to find an unequivocal match," Jake advised. "The lab techs could hit pay dirt on the first sweep. Or, they could go through 95% of the contents before they got a match. And there's no guarantee they'll even find one. But if they do, they're certified and, providing their expenses are paid, will testify. The examination will be done in a forensics laboratory. If they find a cat or rat hair in each source, to prove that they came from the same cat or rat, they'll have to do a DNA analysis. That's not cheap. There would be less convincing testimony of a match if they did micro-analysis of the chemistry of two inorganic samples. You're better off asking for human or animal hair matches."

Sylvia nodded her head and gave a "thumb's up" approval. "Everything's contingent on our getting the gel," Sensei said. "If we get it, as we hope, tomorrow morning, I'll have it on a plane to Honolulu by noon."

George had a question. "Jake, can you get phone records? We can't get them here without a court order; and if we apply for one, we alert too many people to what we're doing. It could be dangerous for us. We need to know who an antique dealer named Ezra Zhen has been talking to. And three museum officials, too. I'll ask our client here to give you the names and phone numbers. Whatever it costs, we'll pay. The danger warrants it."

When all the information had been given to Jake, the call ended and Sensei brought everyone up to date about the Hong Kong Customs' agent who was on her way there.

"Miss Sonya Lee of Hong Kong Customs is coming in tomorrow, before noon. I hope we can deliver the dirt and gel boxes to air freight by the time I pick her up. She was on her way to the airport and will be calling me with her encoded pre-paid cell number any minute now." He looked at his watch, got up, and pushed his chair back to the table. "I might as well go up to the bedroom and wait for her call."

"Code?" George laughed. "What is it with Sonya Lee? Doesn't she trust technology?"

Sensei feigned indignation. "She trusts technology. It's people she doesn't trust. Her training is so bizarre. She studies handwriting analysis and body language. And she's a crack shot with a rifle or a handgun."

"Yes," Sylvia teased, "but can she tie knots or pitch a tent? Was she ever a boy scout?"

"Yes... in a British troop in Hong Kong," he grinned, "and she can handle explosives. I don't know how she is with a bow and arrow or camping out in the woods."

"If she was a scout in Hong Kong," Sylvia noted, "she wouldn't have had much experience camping in the wild."

"Something tells me," George teased, "that Sonya wouldn't be much good on a camping trip."

"Not outside the tent, anyway," Sensei winked.

George teased, "I'm gonna tell Sonya you said that."

"You do, and you won't be just 'cultivating the poise of a dead man.'"

Sensei lay on his bed and waited for Sonya's call. At precisely nine o'clock, the appointed hour, his phone rang. He had his pencil and paper ready. The code was a simple one. Using the standard names for giving letters of the alphabet, and assigning two names per number, he had already written:

0 =Alpha, Bravo; 1=Charlie, Delta; 2=Echo, Foxtrot; 3=Golf, Hotel; 4=India, Juliet; 5=Kilo, Lima; 6=Mike, November; 7=Oscar, Papa; 8=Quebec, Romeo; 9=Sierra, Tango.

He had no need to write Uniform, Victor, Whiskey, Xray, Yankee, Zulu. His phone rang. He answered, and with no word of greeting, Sonya said, "Bravo; Delta; Charlie; Romeo; Lima; Foxtrot," and continued to dictate her new number. Using the same alpha-numeric code, he gave her his new number and almost immediately his prepaid cell rang. They laughed. It was such a simple and almost childish code, but it worked.

Half an hour later Sensei came down to the kitchen with the news from Hong Kong that the others were waiting to hear - the results of Sonya Lee's initial inquiry. "Sonny says that she thinks the Hawaiian - Cheng Lu who apparently held Herb Kalahele's wife and kid hostage - is a boss or maybe 'the' boss in the drug operation. It is not a large ring. 'Lean but choice' describes the small clientele who are supplied."

George shook his head. "Does she know the route they follow?"

"First, she says the shipment was probably pure heroin that had been processed in Thailand or Burma - that's Myanmar. Their agent, who is probably a reputable import-export merchant of some kind, accepts delivery of the heroin and then, in Bangkok, he goes to a reputable antique dealer and buys a jar or two. He asks the dealer to ship the empty jar to his import-export company office in Songkhla or some other port city on the Southeast coast of Thailand. He specifies that it must be extremely well packed in sawdust and a heavy wooden crate. He takes the heroin and drives down to Songhkla and gets his jar. It is an in-country shipment and doesn't involve Customs.

"Sonya thinks that when the agent receives the shipment in Songhkla, he has all the legitimate labels from the antique dealer - the bill of lading, and so on. He puts the heroin in the jar and repackages it - without the heavy sawdust - in as much clear ballistics gel that will keep the weight equal. That might mean that he uses lighter weight wood on the crate's sides that do not contain pasted-on labels. If the labels on the package are damaged he just duplicates them and even the official stamps... same numbers, but he alters or he adds destination information that consigns the jars to the U.S. or Canada. Using his own license information he acts as if the shipment merely passed through Songhkla on its way to the U.S. or Canada. In other words, he is merely the middleman.

"The second way that they could do this would be to buy a jar from a reputable dealer in Singapore and have it shipped to Canada or the U.S. in care of him in Songhkla or some other port city in Thailand. Same deal.

"Sonya doesn't know if he uses a special shipping line. If the shipment were ever questioned, an expert could look through the plastic bag of gel. He could read the Reign Marks and so on. The legitimate dealer's paperwork would likely be enough for Customs to decline to melt the gel."

"A few kilos doesn't sound like a big operation," Terrell Maitlin said.

George explained, "Profit is probably not the only consideration. Their market must be an exclusive one. A few kilos at a time doesn't sound like much, but big shipments involve many small people and that's where the problems come in. This operation can fly under the radar. So few people are involved that they have little to worry about. Everybody is so reputable. Even Cheng Lu is a respectable citizen. If a man is willing to do the manual labor himself - and I assume that these men are - he exponentially narrows his chances of being caught."

"The person we need to find," Sensei noted, "is the consignee. Who the hell specifically was the shipment sent to? Sonya wants us to try to find out whether Sylvia saw the name and just doesn't remember, or whether she saw the label and there was no name on it. That would mean that the recipient at the museum removed it before selling it to Ezra. But there's a problem. Sonny does not want us to involve King County police or the DEA. She asked me if I wanted her to take over the investigation since we're not supposed to interfere in an active police investigation."

Sylvia Maitlin again sat on the floor at her husband's feet. "Doesn't she trust them? If not, I don't blame her one bit. What have they done so far? Nothing. We could have been killed. And besides, there is no active police investigation."

"So tell us, Sylvia," Sensei asked, "do you recall if there was a name that you just can't remember or that there was no name at all?"

"I think there was a name. I didn't make a point of remembering it."

"If you read it, it is there in your memory banks. Let me tell you a little Zen story. Once a novice went to visit his master to ask when he could expect to attain enlightenment. The master replied, "When you came here this evening, on which side of the door did you leave your slippers?" The novice cannot remember... he can guess, but he cannot recall. The master says, "When you can tell me on which side of the door you left your slippers, you'll be enlightened." Some people think that the novice needed to cultivate a photographic memory, that this is what being mindful is all about - being conscious of every detail around you. But it doesn't mean that at all. The human brain records everything it sees and hears regardless of whether our ego-consciousness is interested in it or not. It's there in the mind."

George picked up the explanation. "A Zen adept can enter his memory banks and access any of that unprocessed information. But more to the point, so can anyone under the guidance of a hypnotist. We often see this done when, for example, someone who sees the license number of a getaway car of a bank robbery, but can't remember it. The police will have him hypnotized and he'll spit out the license plate number. It has been in his brain, but not in his ego-conscious memory."

"Maybe we'll get lucky and when we enter Ezra's work room we'll find the crate's lid propped up against the wall; but if we aren't lucky, can we take you to a shrink who does hypnosis and ask him to try to get the writing on the label out of your brain?"

"Sure," Sylvia replied. "I know a good psychiatrist in town, here. As a last resort I can call him and if it's ok, we can see him about it."

I'll call Sonya right away and ask for her opinion," Sensei said. "She's probably boarding her flight right now. It's a thirteen- hour flight from Hong Kong. Meanwhile, you can get prepared to have a flat tire outside Ezra Zhen's antique shop in the morning."

George followed Sensei upstairs to the guest room, intending to sleep. He lay on the twin bed and listened to Sensei and Sonya Lee still talking and giggling. He could hear Sonya say, "Go for it, Cowboy! But there's a good chance you'll find the lid when you B&E. You won't need a shrink for her. By the way," she added carefully, "can you enter your memory banks at will?"

"Yes. Yes, I can. And you would be surprised at what I put in that vault."

"Do I have to 'break and enter' to see what you have there?"

He started his giddy talk again.

George rolled his eyes. "I'm going to take a shower. Maybe Sylvia's doctor can mesmerize you… give you the suggestion that you're a eunuch." He was still laughing at Sensei while he showered.

THURSDAY, SEPTEMBER 15, 2011

Sylvia parked a block away from Ezra's shop and let the air out of a rear tire. Then she slowly drove to the shop and parked in front of it. George and Sensei parked on the side street.

Sylvia had purposely dressed in red... Zhen's favorite color. She walked with a carefree and slightly suggestive attitude as she entered the shop. Sensei got out of the SUV and stood in the shadows on the corner of the street so that he could watch the front of Zhen's shop.

In two minutes Sylvia and Zhen came out. He had taken out his cellphone preparing, Sensei thought, to call an auto repair service. But Sylvia touched his cheek and seemed to plead with him. She was, in fact, telling him that it would take too long. She had wanted to keep her ten o'clock appointment and then come back to see what she could buy in his shop to replace the lost ginger jar. She said that her rims locked and she needed a key to remove the tire and unfortunately she had left her purse inside the shop. "Check my spare!" she turned and called as she got to the doorway.

Sylvia entered the shop and went directly to the workroom, found the key, made sure the alarm system was off, unlocked the back door, ran outside to put the key on the fence post, and returned to the shop to get her purse. She was fumbling for her keys as she stepped out onto the pavement. "I'm in such a dither!" she exclaimed, and made "verging on the point of tears" baby eyes at Zhen.

"Don't you be upset. I'm going to help you as soon as I figure this out."

"Maybe I can get us some help. We can't be proud at a time like this." She called George. "I'm at Ezra's. I've got a flat tire. This is such dirty work for a gentleman to do. If you can possibly stop by to help, we would be so appreciative."

Sensei had seen her hand reach up onto the post and deposit the key there. Knowing he had a limited amount of time to enter, he motioned to George to follow him to the fence.

Sensei put the key in his pocket, easily climbed the fence, and entered the kitchen. He found the bag of gel, but the spindle and clip that contained sales and purchase receipts, were not on the desk. He checked the sides of the room for the crate's lid, and not finding it, took the bag of gelatin and left, locking the kitchen door after him. The bag of gelatin was heavier than he imagined and presented a problem in getting it over the cinderblock wall without tearing it. George finally was able to receive it intact and to carry it to the SUV. He and Sensei drove around the block and parked in front of the antique shop.

Sylvia ran up to greet them. "Ezra and I are so appreciative. I don't know what I would have done if he hadn't been here to help me. I was nearly falling apart until he came to my rescue. I'm late for my appointment."

"Don't worry," George said. "You can switch cars with us and we'll handle the flat tire." As she handed him the wheel lock he secretly pressed the back door key into her hand.

"Ezra, darling, could I possibly use your bathroom?" she asked sweetly.

"You don't have to ask," he said with an intimate kind of shyness.

When they returned to the Maitlins' house, George and Sensei found that Sylvia had already delivered the gel bag and was at the gun shop, taking her shooting lesson. Terrell Maitlin had loaded the gel and the dirt into two heavy cardboard boxes ready to be shipped to Honolulu.

Sensei addressed the boxes and fearing that they would be late to meet Sonya, he asked Terrell to take them to the airfreight terminal.

Beryl Tilson had just gotten out of the shower when the office phone's extension rang in her "bedroom-office." She hurried to answer it before the voice-mail kicked on. Dr. Dao Wu of the Philadelphia Art Museum was calling.

"I don't want to bother you unnecessarily with just a gossipy tale, but I heard from a contact I have in the antique porcelain bazaar. I had been hoping to acquire a certain Ming ginger jar. It would have been donated to the museum by one of our benefactors. Unfortunately, someone else got it at auction. Then my contact said a museum near Seattle was going to get it. I asked who was donating it and he said, and I quote, 'some rich dude in Honolulu.' So, that's it, for whatever it's worth."

"When is the shipment going to be made?"

"I have no idea. But the auction was a month ago. I can email you a photo of the jar. It appeared in the catalog. Has Sonya Lee arrived there yet?"

"She's going to Seattle... not Philadelphia. I'll be sure to relay the information you just gave me and if Sonya has any questions, she can call you directly. Do you have a private line?"

Beryl recorded Wu's private number and thanked him for the new lead on the "porcelain wars."

"I'm not going to ask how the investigation is going," Wu replied, "I will say only if the owner ever wants to give that Qing jar a home here in our museum... well, we'd love to have it."

"She may be mad enough at the administrators of her local museum to take you up on that. But thanks for the information. I'll pass it on right now."

George took Beryl's call as Sensei maneuvered his way through the parking area of the terminal. He was not surprised. "Did he say how many jars were in the pipeline?"

"Just one."

"I'm beginning to fear that it might be necessary to do a stealth entry into the museum. If another jar has been shipped, the receiver may be there in the museum repackaging it for smaller deliveries. If it comes inside a gel casing, the receiver may have to dissolve it at night or back in the repair area or basement - if the place has a basement."

"Sensei and you sneak into a museum?" Beryl wondered aloud. "I don't like the sound of that."

"I don't know what we'll do. There are so many tangential avenues. Now that you've heard there may possibly be another shipment in the pipeline, new plans will have to be made. I'm finally going to meet La Belle Sonya. Percy and I are pulling into SeaTac right now to pick her up. When she hears that more heroin may be coming in, she may want to do some investigating, herself. I hate to be a fifth wheel," he said for Sensei's benefit, "but while Percy and Sonya are individually sensible people, when they are together they get sort of high on each other and lose a lot of common sense. Inebriated. They're gonna get each other killed."

"You don't have to tell me. I've been there," Beryl laughed. Just keep an eye on them, and keep me in the loop."

"How's everything at home? I talked to my kids. They're planning a Thanksgiving ski trip."

"So is Jack. I just got him new skis. He and Groff Eckersley are going skiing in Colorado over Thanksgiving. They're also making ski plans for Christmas. Jack, Groff, Lilyanne, and Margaret Cioran of Seattle are going away. This will be Margaret's post-recovery debut. I'll have to get Jack new clothes for the trip. Three of the four can afford to ski anywhere on the planet; but Jack's not in their financial league. I told Groff that he has to respect that, and that I'd be upset if he even offered to pay for Jack. The Ciorans have a ski lodge in Idaho. Stephen Cioran wants them to use it. I hope they take him up on his offer - then Jack won't feel like the 'poor boy' of the group. He can drive up and then won't even have to rent a car."

"So Lilyanne is back from her tour?"

"No... all this was arranged by phone. Groff told me that Lily and Margaret Cioran talk every day. As far as I know, Lilyanne is somewhere in the South Pacific."

"I'm glad to hear she's getting her life back on track."

Sensei parked. "We're here," George said. "Talk to you later." As Sensei got out of the car, George called up Lilyanne's photo on his phone. "Fresh kid!" he said, and, since Sensei was momentarily out of sight, George brushed the photo against his lips and quickly clicked off his iPhone.

Ezra Zhen had returned to his shop, happy that he had been able to assist Sylvia. Instinctively he checked to see that nothing was "out of place."

The display cases were untouched. He went into his workroom. Nothing was amiss with the articles on his desk and on his workbenches. He tested the rear door. It was locked as before. He returned to his workroom and his eye missed seeing something... the bag of gel! It was gone!

A panic momentarily seized him. When had he last seen it? He couldn't remember. So much had happened in the last few days. The bag was too heavy for a woman to lift. That let Sylvia off the list of possible thieves. He went to his ink and brush and lifted the tray. The key was still there exactly as he had left it. Percy and George never entered the building. There was only one inescapable conclusion: someone from the museum must have taken it. But why? Who? How?

Sonya Lee was among the last passengers to emerge from the jetway. To Sensei she looked so stunningly regal that if someone were to say that all the first class, business, and other coach passengers were in her retinue, he would have been believed without question.

Her hair was not visible beneath the black hat that circled her forehead and temples with an extremely wide brim that rose up and then sloped down to cover the right side of her face. On the left side, behind her ear, was a cluster of crimson silk poppies that seemed to peek out from under the hat's brim at her neckline. These were her only decorative objects. She wore no jewelry, but her lipstick matched the poppies' crimson color. Her suit, handbag, and shoes were black and featureless and, Sensei thought, would have been so were they ornate, for any onlooker's attention was fixed upon her face and hat. She also carried a long, silver-handled walking stick.

The sight of her literally took Sensei's breath away. He gasped and stood motionless for a long moment seeing an image that in his mind would petrify and exist forever... a statue... an icon. George nudged him and he breathed again.

She walked towards him, putting her clutch purse under her left arm and the walking stick in her left hand. She extended her right hand and Sensei, dazzled into dumbness, bent over it to kiss it.

George waited for Sensei "to regain consciousness," as he would later describe the response. Perhaps it was Sensei's breath on the perfume on her hand, but George was certain that he could smell the scent that apparently was intoxicating his friend. George nudged him again and he released her fingers.

"Hi, Miss Lee," George said. "I'm George Wagner, his wingman. He needs protection."

Sonya extended her hand, holding it so high that it was clear that she expected him to kiss her hand. He clasped it in his weak right hand, turned her hand over, and kissed her palm. "You are everything he said you were."

The gesture surprised and amused her. "Have you been watching over my personal Zen priest?"

"I watch him as a hawk watches another hawk." George laughed.

"And whom does that hawk watch?"

"You," Sensei said simply.

"See that it stays that way."

"I will not fail."

"Oh, my God!" George groaned. "Let's get out of here."

All the way to the luggage carousel George wondered how Sensei was going to tell Miss Lee that they'd be walking through a sewer on their way to break into a museum.

Sensei, George, Sonya, and Sylvia sat in the living room-gallery and discussed the next move they should make. Sonya vetoed calling any psychiatrist to probe Sylvia's memory. "It's not worth the risk. Doctors have nurses and receptionists and clerks. The more people who know a secret, the sooner the secret becomes common knowledge."

"As long as we're not going to waste time on shrinks," Sylvia turned to Sonya, "why don't you and I go upstairs and I'll get you 'situated,' as they say, in your new accommodations." The two women went upstairs with Sensei trailing behind them, carrying Sonya Lee's suitcase.

Before Sensei reached the top of the stairs, his phone rang. He put the suitcase down on the step and answered Jake Renquist's call.

"I'm ready to fax the material you wanted. Are you able to receive it?"

"Yes... go right ahead. What's the price?"

"5K."

"Cheap at twice the price. Thanks, J.R. You want it in cash?"

"Cash is better."

"I'll fed-ex it this afternoon... along with the other two grand I owe you. Ciao."

As Sensei finished carrying the suitcase to Sonya's room he could hear the fax machine bell ring in Terrell Maitlin's "man cave."

The telephone LUDS for Zhen, Peng, Banning, and Gao came in. The laptop that George brought had a reverse directory for nearly all of the area codes listed. Beryl, having more comprehensive equipment, checked the others in their Philadelphia office.

In the second week of August a group of calls had been made to U.S. and Canadian consular offices. Sonya was able to determine which merchant ship had unloaded its cargo from Singapore on August 4th. The manifest was published and from this she was able to isolate several crates that were shipped to the Wai Neng Museum. The shipper was the Smith-Cheung Antiques Company of Singapore.

Between the calls made to the consulates were calls to travel agents. And then, from those distant areas the private cellphones of Doctors Peng or Gao made phone calls, assuring that they had gone to the area of the consulate.

Sonya took the lead in the discussion. "It's evident that the contraband was received here and then distributed to various consular officers in the U.S. and Canada. It's significant that consulates as far away as Montreal and Miami were in this loop."

"Why would a diplomat want to get involved with drugs?" Maitlin asked. "I can't imagine a person who has risen so high in the public's esteem that he's been selected to represent his country abroad - while at the same time he's a low-life scum who would deal drugs or be some kind of drug mule."

"What you need to understand," George answered him, trying to be gentle, "is that there are always people who through no fault of their own - or perhaps as a result of adolescent foolishness - have become dependent upon opiates. These people can be intelligent, educated, and financially successful - good citizens, folks we're proud to know.

"A diplomat won't risk embarrassing his country by being caught buying illegal drugs or even getting prescriptions filled for opiates. But he or someone in his family may need the narcotics. So this is as clean an operation as you can find - outside medical circles. A well-meaning diplomat may feel that by helping his friends, relatives, or even visiting businessmen to get these drugs without the fear of public exposure, he's doing his country a great service. He rationalizes his actions and doesn't understand addiction and that peculiar need of addicts to make new addicts. He thinks he's some kind of drug-delivering 'Robin Hood'."

"Who would have thought so much trouble could come from one old jar?" Terrell Maitlin grew silent.

Sonya was firm. "Not all of these consulates are PRC - People's Republic of China. The trouble that the traffickers have taken to keep this operation secret is an indication that none of the governments involved would tolerate it. Otherwise, they'd just move the drugs through diplomatic pouches. It would be nice to think that there is only an altruistic motive behind the effort, but we all know better. There are undoubtedly many licentious activities involved. We can only hope that there isn't some Inca civilization artwork being donated to Indigenous people's museums here in the hemisphere."

"Altruistic coca traffickers," George said. "What's next?"

"What we have to do is find out when that Ming jar is due to arrive. We need to get evidence that it contains heroin and is being distributed to consular officials around the country. For all we know it's already here."

"You can operate in an official capacity when you're standing on consular land. Perce and I can't involve ourselves in the operation beyond presenting evidence that it's taking place; but tracking drugs across country is the DEA's job."

"Suppose the drugs are here," Sylvia wondered. "How long would they stay around?"

"Probably not long. This is another way of saying that we have to get started tracking it immediately. Tomorrow we can go down to the docks and see if we can get any information. You game?"

"You bet I am."

"Just a minute," Sensei and Terrell simultaneously said. Sensei stood up. "Terrell and I will go down to the docks. You two will stay here. And the matter isn't up for discussion." He turned to Terrell. "Right?"

"Absolutely," Terrell agreed. "Sylvia, we appreciate your enthusiasm. Dumpster diving is one thing. Hanging out at the docks is out of the question."

Sonya put her hand on Sylvia's arm. "It's all right," she said. "When they fail, we can go down. That way you can get your afternoon shooting lesson in while they waste time trying. By the way, how did you do at your morning lesson?"

"8-22. I'm improving rapidly."

"Tell us about the museum's layout," George asked. "And that odd room stuck on the rear."

"Our part of town," Sylvia explained, "was founded by Chinese gandy dancers and other railroad employees. They brought their families over. This was in the 1920s and 30s. There was a creek... Tsao Chi... that flowed downhill and was their source of fresh water. The first buildings were a stable and a restaurant. After the restaurant burned down in the 1950s, it was rebuilt in the sturdy construction you see today; but it wasn't profitable so the Wai Neng museum bought the building.

"Aside from the individual houses, the next buildings were a grocery store and a school and then a bunch of cabins - the early form of motels. The motel and the restaurant needed clean linens and so a Chinese laundry followed. But the problem of water was enormous. The practice of dumping sewage into the creek was causing a war. The biggest polluters were the restaurant and the stable and then the laundry. They happened to be on the same side of the creek, so they pooled their resources and dug a sewer... a tunnel, and they diverted some water from the creek higher up the mountain and let it run through this sewer and then rejoin the creek half a mile downstream. The whole half-mile sewer line - which a person can walk inside - is quite nice since no more sewage is dumped into it. The water and sewer lines were replaced as the city grew and encompassed the town. But by the time they did that the atomic bomb threats of the cold war made the old sewer line a perfect fallout shelter.

"The museum kitchen - which used to be part of the restaurant's kitchen - has two back doors. A big one that functions as a loading dock - which is the door they still use - and another small door that leads into that room that's stuck on the back of the building. Inside that room is a manhole cover in the floor that allows access to the old sewer line. When the restaurant stopped dumping garbage down the hole and a municipal garbage truck began to collect it, they'd leave the garbage dumpster in that room so it wouldn't stink up the area.

"But when the restaurant became a museum, they bricked up the outside entrance to the room and kept the cleaned-out sewer line as a fallout shelter. I think they also considered that in a nuclear war they could put valuable art objects down there for safe keeping, and then times changed and they more or less forgot about it. The only time I know that they used it for anything else was to store champagne down there while they prepared for a big museum fund raising party - I was the chairwoman for the party. As I've said, the creek water that flows through the line is relatively clean. Since I was on the fund-raising committee I knew where the key to the small kitchen door that leads into the room is kept. So technically, if you want to get into the workroom or the administrative offices, you can access it through the old sewer and just come up into that room through the manhole, and then if the door's deadbolt is unlocked, and the door's connection to the alarm system is turned off, you can just go in."

"How much water flows through the line?" George asked.

"In the dry season there's a trickle of water; but when it rains, a substantial amount of water will flow through it. The sewer line serves as a run-off channel and takes a lot of pressure off the creek when the flow is torrential. That's why they never sealed it off. This is the start of the rainy season, so if you wanted to access it now, you'd need some kind of dry gear, like a diver's hooded 'dry' suit - they're a lot easier to get on and off unlike wet suits."

"We'd need to know how many people are working on the gel dissolving and drug distribution work. What kind of guards are on duty while the staff is away?" George asked.

Sylvia answered. "At night and on the weekend they have one man mostly, but another one spells him. The guard who will probably be on is Wilfred Ruggles, a senile ladies' man. He thinks all women hunger for him."

"He's an old rake," Terrell said. "Ogles all the girls."

"What's a gandy dancer?" Sensei asked.

"A fellow who lays railroad tracks," Terrell said. "They would secure the iron track onto the wooden ties and make sure the lines were straight."

George interrupted. "Let me see if I understand this." He pursed his lips and tried to visualize Sylvia's plan. "You think we can enter the old sewer system someplace, walk to the manhole behind the museum, and then enter the museum through that old kitchen door and then catch them in the act of handling the heroin?"

"Well... yes."

"How far away from the Museum will we enter the sewer?"

"The entrance where the Chinese laundry once was is now in the middle of someone's lawn. But the stable's entrance is now beside a park. We could park on the street right there. It's about a football field's length uphill to the Museum."

Terrell Maitlin was adamant. "I'm not going with you to break into the museum. And you are not going, either."

Sylvia patted his hand. "It's all right, dear. You can drive the getaway van."

"Preposterous!" Maitlin snarled. "And what will you do with the guard? Shoot him?"

"It's a valid question," George noted. "Just what do you have in mind for the guard?"

"The guard," Sylvia said seductively, "is a ladies man. He's in his sixties but he has the libido of a seventeen year old. Wilfred Ruggles...

the name lets you think he's a milquetoast kind of guy, but he's far from it. He prowls those aisles at night when he's alone and gets all kinds of sexual inspirations. A secretary once encountered him at night when she went into her office for something and he practically propositioned her.

"Anyway, Terrell can call the receptionist's private desk phone and when the guard answers, as he usually does, he can ask him if I'm there yet. Wilfred will say that he doesn't know why I would be there at all, and then Terrell can say, 'Oh... dear... I've spoiled the surprise. She's bringing you a cake she made, trying out a new recipe for your birthday. She heard you say you liked chocolate cake and thought you'd enjoy it. She feels so bad about causing the museum such bad publicity that she wants to make it up to you.'" She rubbed Terrell's hand. "If the guard pushes it, Terrell can say that I'm regretful - but not sufficiently regretful to deal with Banning, Peng, and Gao, yet. I'll get him to let me in the front door... not the big revolving door but another one the staff uses. I'll find an excuse to go back to the kitchen area and unlock the door; and then I'll keep him busy while you guys enter the kitchen and access the workrooms. How's that?"

"And then what?" Terrell demanded.

"I told you. I'll be eating some cake with him... gabbing over a little drinky-poo. We'll be in the front of the museum. Just don't be noisy. Oh... remind me to bring my iPod player. I'll put some sexy music on to cover any noise you make."

"When do you plan to do this?" Sensei scratched his head - a gesture that indicated that he was not quite comfortable with the plan that had been put before him.

"Anytime. Do you have to get back East?"

"No. But who all will be going through the sewer?"

Sonya Lee answered, definitively. "You and I. We should bring a dry suit for Sylvia in case she has to escape through the sewer line."

Terrell Maitlin looked sternly at his wife and objected. "I can't believe that my own wife has concocted this harebrained scheme. It's one thing to get a gun. But now you're a cat burglar? Or would that be a 'rat burglar' - wading through sewers?"

"Who knows," Sylvia retorted, "I may find some phony porcelain pieces 'aging' down there."

She checked her watch. "Time for my afternoon shooting lesson. Sonny, will you come with me? Maybe you can give me some pointers."

Sensei stood up. "We have to Fed-ex $7,000 in cash to Honolulu. When we get back we can go down to the docks and see what we can learn."

"You go ahead," Terrell said to George. "I'll hold the fort down here."

"We'll be wearing diver's gear," Sonya said. "This is going to be exciting."

At the gun shop, Sylvia asked her for an opinion about her choice of weapon. Miss Lee pronounced the Beretta "perfect."

"Are you interested in buying a gun?" the salesman asked Sonya.

"No. I already have one... a Colt Mustang."

"Need any lessons?"

"We all can use instruction," she said. "*Ancora Imparo*."

"Well," said the salesman, "Come on back to the shooting range and we'll see how much instruction you require."

Sylvia faced the target and emptied the 10-round magazine but hit the target paper only twice. Sonya took the Beretta from her and put another clip in it. "In my opinion, you've got a depth perception problem. Your binocular-stereo vision is off." She pointed at a logo that was on the wall. "You are right handed which means your left eye is probably dominant. Put your left thumb straight out in front of you until it visually covers that logo." As Sylvia raised her arm and positioned her thumb over the logo in her line of vision, Sonya took an envelope from her purse and covered Sylvia's right eye. "Is the thumb still covering the logo?" It was. Sonya then covered Sylvia left eye. "Has the thumb moved?"

"My God!" Sylvia exclaimed. "It moved completely off the logo."

"Here's what I think. If you had all the time in the world to learn to shoot properly, you could practice this frontal stance until you strengthened your weak eye or mentally learned to compensate for it. But you don't have time. So we have to try another technique. I personally prefer the lateral posture to the frontal. Try it this way," she said, turning sideways to the target. "Take a fencer's posture. You are less of a target when you're standing edge-on, like a knife blade. You can even bend your knees a little - especially if you think you might have to run or move in any way or if you have a recoil problem. Sight down the barrel with one eye... something you're not supposed to do when you take a frontal stance. If you're right handed, shoot with your left hand and sight with your left eye. Close your right eye and point the weapon with your left arm stretched out. If you're left handed, do the opposite. Use the gun-sight to align your eye to the target. Make a fist with your unused hand and put it on your hip... just like a fencer."

"Show me," Sylvia giggled eagerly.

The salesman put a stop to the lesson. "Girls... this is not a playground. We don't teach fencing postures and keeping one eye shut. You need to learn the proper technique. These are serious weapons!"

"'Girls'?" Sonya repeated, looking through him as though he had suddenly become clear glass. She continued to look back at him as she turned sideways and put her left fist on her hip and pointed the gun at the target. Then she turned her head, aligned the sight at the man's outline on the paper target and put five slugs into his painted heart. She transferred the gun to her left hand, turned, and shot the target with equal accuracy. "You try it," she said to Sylvia.

Sylvia was thrilled by the display. "I will never tire of showing men up for their 'misogynistic stupidities,'" she said, slapping another clip into the weapon. "I hold my dinner fork in my left hand. Why should I not hold my Beretta in the same hand?" She managed to put five bullets into the paper. She did not hit the heart but, as Sonya assured her, "Your first shot would have brought him down. You hit his left eye."

"And you like your Colt Mustang?" Sylvia asked.

"Yes. Very much."

"Fine," Sylvia said to the salesman. "I'll take one of them, too."

They returned home to discover that George and Sensei had gone to the docks and did not know where to begin to look for any ships that had arrived from Singapore. They had returned without any information at all.

FRIDAY, SEPTEMBER 16, 2011

Sonya Lee and Sylvia Maitlin did not look like sisters, but they immediately acted like sisters. Sylvia insisted upon showing Sonya her porcelain collection. She opened the cases and allowed Sonya to pick up the pieces and inspect them. No one else had ever been given the privilege.

George, Sensei, and Terrell Maitlin sat speechlessly at the kitchen table as the two women reviewed the plan, laughing and talking about rats and fecal material as they slathered butter on their toast and hot sauce on their omelettes.

"The plan will work," Miss Lee announced to the men. "It will be dangerous. If the heroin has arrived they will distribute it immediately. They won't keep it on the premises. We have no time to lose."

Terrell Maitlin was not awed by the Hong Kong agent or the plan. "I'm appalled to think that the two of you are serious about breaking and entering a museum. And frankly, making sexual overtures to an old fool like Wilfred Ruggles to facilitate an illegal entry is, and ought to be, beneath you."

Sonya tried to ease his concern. "I realize that there are parts of the plan that are crude, but we simply don't have time to refine them."

Maitlin bristled. "Does no one have any common sense? Think about what you propose to do. How will you make your escape? Run out into the shed and jump into the sewer? And if you're followed--"

"Terrell! Stop your nonsense!" Sylvia had ceased to be patient. "We'll probably end up by calling the police. And if we had to wade through the sewer for a few yards, so what? It isn't you who'll be getting wet!"

"I want no part of this!" Terrell fumed. He pushed back the kitchen chair and as it scraped on the tile floor, he childishly said to his wife, "and you can take Miss Lee with you for your next gun-toting lesson!"

He left the kitchen and went into his den.

George and Sensei did not want to get involved in the discussion, but if they were going to pursue the case, they had to make certain preparations. "We have to rent a van," George said, "and three hooded dry suits."

"Why don't we do that now," Sensei suggested.

"No," Sonya objected. "First we have to find out if the shipment of the Ming jar Beryl found out about has been delivered to the museum. You, I believe, insisted on doing that."

"Yes," Sensei said. "But we couldn't locate the ship so we didn't know which Customs' office to go to."

"Let me give you the latest 'vessel arrival' information. You can check the Customs office closest to the ships." She looked up the latest "in port" arrivals on her "official" phone and slid the phone across the table to Sensei. "Sylvia and I will go to her morning lesson and meet you back here. Then we can make further plans depending on what you've learned." She turned to Sylvia. "They won't learn anything."

Sensei and George left to go down to the docks again to see what they could learn about ships that had arrived from Singapore. While George waited in the car, Sensei went in to the Customs' office. The Customs' agent was polite but he asked that a form be filled out, stating shipper and consignee, and a description of the freight as well as a bill of lading number and shipping invoice. Sensei thanked him and left.

He returned to the Maitlins' home just as Sylvia and Sonya returned from the morning lesson. Sylvia was excited. The three-day waiting period was up and the gun shop had given her "her very own" Beretta. She would not get her Colt until the following week.

When Sensei explained that he was unable to get any "inside" information about a ship that had last stopped in Singapore, Sonya tapped Sylvia on the shoulder. "Put some 'butch' clothing on... maybe comb your hair back with some mousse. You can be my pimp if we have to question the longshoremen. But I should get what we need from Customs." She made sure she had gum in her purse and went upstairs to get a "street-walker's" wig from her suitcase. "Let's get down to the docks and see what kind of trouble we can get into." She turned to Sensei. "When we get the information, I'll call you and you'll know whether or not to go out and get the van and the dry suits."

Sylvia, her denim cowboy jacket's collar turned up, tried to strike a James Dean pose as she sat in the car and waited for Sonya who, looking like an executive secretary, burst into the Customs' office. "Please tell me I'm not too late," Sonya said, affecting a desperate tone, "and that we don't have to wait till Monday! Did the museum get its shipment from Singapore? I was delayed with car trouble and my phone just died."

The clerk turned around and asked, "Did they pick those crates up?"

"As far as I know, they got both of them. There was a Chinese guy here an hour ago looking for information about a shipment to the museum."

"Tall? Slim guy? Short hair?"

"Yeah," the agent said.

Sonya affected a conspiratorial air. "He's the bloody fool that lost track of the shipment. He was going to take care of everything. I was a fool to entrust him with the job. You know what JFK said, she smiled and winked at him, "'Never send a boy to do a man's job. Send a woman.' But I want to thank you," she said, pausing in the doorway. "You saved my neck." She left the office.

Sylvia asked, "Where is it?"

"They got several crates from Singapore. We're on. They'll be cutting the stuff now." She called Sensei and told him to proceed with the van and the dry suits.

"Now," Sylvia said, "I've got to bake a cake. Let's pray that Wilfred is on duty tonight."

Terrell Maitlin was repentant after his childish pique. "Would you think that I was a lunatic if I bought them night vision goggles?" he asked George.

"No... That's a long stretch of sewer," George said. "Not only that, but if the lights are off in the museum and the windows are covered, it will be dark inside. They would have to use flashlights and nothing can make a person a target the way carrying a flashlight can."

"Are they expensive?"

"About three thousand dollars a pop."

"Ouch," Maitlin said. "Oh, what the hell. She's got a few good years left in her." He left with Sensei and George to go to the Sport and Survivor supply store.

It was still daylight as George and Terrell, using a camcorder, went to the museum and photographed all the cars in the parking lot and in the immediate vicinity. They would return home and check out the license numbers. Then, before the actual sewer trek began, they'd drive around again to see what changes had taken place. They wanted recordings of as much museum traffic as they could get.

Terrell got immediate responses when he ran down the list of license plate owners with the police department. "Does this come under 'color of office?' he asked George. "It's the first time I've ever tried to get anything done that was remotely connected with a crime."

They made a final pass of the museum. One new vehicle had arrived in the parking lot. Trees obscured an area between the car and one of the museum's side doors. George got out and strolled past the car and relayed the license number to Terrell who called it in. The car, a Toyota, was registered to Harriet Yong, a local woman. A search of her name found nothing.

George had looked in the car's windows and saw that the back seat was covered with boxes and garments. At most, George thought, the car had carried only two people.

Terrell parked the van beside the manhole cover at the edge of the park. "It's happening. It's really happening. I'm a former police commissioner and I'm sitting out here in a rented van with two people in diver's suits and wading boots carrying a backpack that contains a suit for my wife for when she escapes after having participated in a museum break-in and seducing an on-duty guard. And I was worried about being criticized for buying a fake jar."

"It's time to drive me down to the museum," Sylvia said. "When I get inside you can call Wilfred," she reminded him. "You know what to say."

"First let me see the two of them go down the manhole. Maybe the cover has been welded shut."

Sonya and Sensei jumped out of the van and, using a small crowbar's foot, opened the cover. Sensei went down first and adjusted his night vision goggles. Sonya followed, carrying the backpack that contained a camera and the third hooded dry suit and goggles.

Terrell drove the quarter-mile to the museum and let Sylvia and her picnic basket out of the van. He parked in the shadows and watched her ring the bell on the employee entrance door. Wilfred Ruggles opened the door and, as though she were a call-girl he had summoned, stuck his head out to see who might possibly have seen her enter.

Terrell called the museum's unlisted reception desk number. Wilfred Ruggles answered the call.

"Mr. Ruggles," Maitlin said, trying to sound like a concerned and suspicious husband, "this is Terrell Maitlin. Has my wife arrived there yet to see you? She said she was taking you a birthday present."

"I think she's here now—" Ruggles said as Sylvia frantically gestured "No!"

"Sorry, my mistake," Ruggles said as she went up to him and made a face of disapproval at the telephone. "If I see her I'll tell her you called."

"Was he checking up on me?" she asked, intimating that her husband's call had been prompted by jealousy.

"What's the man got to be jealous of?" Ruggles asked.

"Any beefcake that comes near me gets him feelin' insecure." She was amused by her own brazenness. Beefcake? She nearly laughed aloud.

Ruggles evidently thought the description apt. "I try to keep in shape. Honey, you cannot imagine the machismo... that's what it's called... machismo a man like me feels especially when he's in a place like this alone. A beautiful doll like you is heaven-sent! Your old man said you were bringing me a birthday present. Girl... my birthday ain't for another couple of months."

"I said 'birthday' just to keep him calm. I've caused the museum so much trouble lately. I'm sorry for that. So it's really a peace offering." She stroked his arm.

"A peace offering or a 'piece' offering," Ruggles said with smutty adolescent slyness.

"Why Wilfred Ruggles! You are a beast!" She led him to the couch and turned on her iPod player to a bossa nova album. She sat down and opened the picnic basket and produced the loaf-shaped cake on which she had inscribed, "Making amends." She also lifted a bottle of champagne from the basket. "We can have a tiny taste of this 1999 Bollinger after we have some of this mousse cake. You do like sweets?" She stood up. "Problem is... he expects that you'll take the cake home with you, so I couldn't bring any paper plates. I know where they keep them in the cafeteria. You open the bottle and I'll be right back. I did manage to bring plastic forks."

"Did you bring glasses?" Wilfred called. "And I hope nobody in the back workroom hears me opening the bottle. It'll sound like a gun shot."

"In the basket is a towel. That ought to muffle the sound. You'll find two plastic cups in there. That was the best I could manage."

Sylvia went into the kitchen and took the kitchen door key ring out of the old chef's desk, turned off the security alarm for the door and unlocked it, trying it to be sure it was not stuck or nailed shut. She grabbed two paper plates from a cabinet and made her way back to Wilfred Ruggles who had opened the champagne and was amusingly dancing with the bottle.

The night vision goggles were useful only in the area around the manhole. As they walked fifty feet ahead, Sensei stopped walking and touched Sonya's arm. "Let's use the flashlight," he said. He lifted his goggles up to his forehead and waited for her to do the same before he turned on the flashlight.

"Ok. Let there be light!" Sonya quipped, and they proceeded by flashlight to the museum's sewer entrance.

The sewer's interior had been lined with glazed ceramic tiles. After the municipal authorities had constructed its own water and sewage system, the owners went into the half-mile long sewage channel and with long-handled brushes scrubbed it clean so that the channel could be used for emergency purposes and also that it wouldn't become a breeding ground for rats. Here and there a tree root did manage to penetrate the concrete and tile wall, but otherwise only organic debris, mainly leaves and twigs, entered the channel at the diversion point of the creek. Periodically the owners of the laundry - the business nearest the end of the sewer line - would have to remove any accumulation that threatened to block the flowing water from rejoining the creek and would force the water to seep out the manhole cover near the park.

Sensei and Sonya reached the museum's exit, took off their dry suits and left them hanging on the lateral supports of the ladder along with Sylvia's "escape" goggles and dry suit. They did take their goggles to be able to make their way through the darkened areas of the museum without having to use flashlights, although Sensei did bring a flashlight and Sonya, a penlight. She also carried tools and her Colt inside a fanny pack.

They climbed the ladder, entered the enclosed "exterior room" and pushed the kitchen door open.

They knew the layout of the rear of the building. The kitchen, which had originally been large and contained a pantry and much culinary equipment, was now partitioned into a cafeteria and a large storage and repair room, and finally, on the other end, a few executive offices.

The kitchen was dark and they slowly advanced to the repair and storage room at the rear of the building. They could hear people speaking Chinese and could see three of them clearly in the brightly lit room. There were two men and a woman. They all spoke Chinese natively. Sonya held up her hand, signaling Sensei to stop so that she could listen. The men talked about two jars. One was supposed to be a fake and the other genuine. They did not know which was which. The woman, who was sitting at a table and had her back to Sonya, said she didn't know, either. A fourth voice spoke. Sensei thought it sounded like Joseph Peng but he could not see him or understand what he had said. Sonya did understand. She whispered, "They're arguing about phony and real pieces. Only one of them - a man sitting at a desk - knows which is which. It sounds like he's the boss." She strained to look at the third man. She saw - but had no way of recognizing - that it was Joseph Peng.

The first man suddenly spoke English without an accent. "Why the hell is it necessary for me to drive the shit across the border? If he comes down, they can't search him. If I get stopped, it's twenty years."

The other man, speaking with a Chinese accent, agreed with him. They were clearly complaining to the man at the desk. "They got thousands of miles unguarded border with Canada. Why we stick our necks out and look like terrorists…risk getting ourselves searched? He came all the way from Ottawa. Why can't he go little farther and come this side? It's crazy."

Peng ordered the first man, "Go check the bathroom. See how much of that gelatin is still on the jar."

Sonya had been walking ahead of Sensei. They had been threading their way through various sawdust-filled barrels, boxes of unidentifiable junk, and crates. Neither of them knew that the bathroom that serviced the cafeteria also served the workers and the administrative staff. It was located just behind them. They could hear the man's footsteps coming nearer. Suddenly he stopped and switched on an overhead light, seeing them standing not twenty feet in front of him. "Hey!" he yelled. "Guys! Get out here! We've got visitors!" Immediately the woman and the second man rushed to his aid.

"Two are probably the ninja types who invaded the Maitlins," Sensei said, letting Sonya know that they were probably trained martial artists as he moved in front of her. "Take it easy," Sensei called. "We can explain everything!"

Joseph Peng pushed aside a hanging tapestry and recognized Sensei. "It's the private investigator Maitlin hired. Capture them! They cannot be allowed to leave." He showed them a revolver that he carried. "But no noise!"

Sonya tried to maneuver herself away from Sensei to spread out the target and force their attackers to divide their attention; but the woman recognized what Sonya was attempting to do. She took a small canister of mace from her pocket and, in two running steps, she leaped and kicked Sonya's chest hard, forcing her to stumble backwards as mace was sprayed towards her. Some of the mace made contact with one of Sonya's eyes and she yelped at the searing pain. As Sensei turned to help her, a metal rod cracked him on the shoulder and head and he fell unconscious at her feet. Blood gushed from his head wound.

The second man picked him up by his collar, looked at the head wound, and dropped him back onto the floor. "This guy finished."

Joseph Peng said, "Bring them both back to the workroom."

Sonya Lee was picked up and carried to the room. The woman bound her wrists and ankles and unbuckled her fanny pack and tossed it onto her worktable. Sensei was dragged back by his collar and left in a heap on the floor by Peng's desk.

"A Chinese chick," the second man said. "Know who pay big for piece of ass like this? That stockbroker in Vancouver."

"Keep your mind on your work," Peng snarled. "Go see if there are any more visitors out there."

"I don't think it's smart we waste this babe."

Sonya cried for water to wash her eye out, and the woman got an empty pitcher and filled it at the sink. "Put your head back," she commanded, and when Sonya did, she poured water onto her eyes.

"More," Sonya begged.

She returned to the sink, filled the pitcher, and came back to yank Sonya's hair back and pour the entire pitcher onto her face. The water went up Sonya's nose and she began to cough and choke.

"That's enough!" Peng shouted. "Wipe off her face and put a gag in her mouth. I don't want to hear her whining or warning anybody. See if there are others with them in the museum."

The girl raised her hand, signaling that they be quiet. They listened and heard the faint sound of music coming from the front of the building. "Watch her," Peng ordered the girl as he searched Sensei's pockets.

The two men crept to the front of the building and approached Sylvia and Wilfred Ruggles who were laughing at a dirty joke Wilfred had just told. The two men leapt into the area, startling them.

Wilfred assumed that Sylvia's husband had hired them. "What the hell is this?" he demanded. "Did you set me up?"

"No!" she yelled, reaching her right hand into her purse for her Beretta. One of the men grabbed Sylvia's hair and shoved her against the wall, her hand still inside the purse. Wilfred was struggling to undo the snap on his holster. As he stood there, confused, the same steel rod that had felled Sensei now whacked his thighs and he toppled onto the floor, writhing in pain. Sylvia's right index finger was on the trigger. The Beretta was ready to be fired, but her back was against the wall, and she was momentarily confused. Should she use her left hand? Should she turn sideways and try to shoot with her right? Try a frontal shot? She knew her dismal record of hitting what she aimed at. Relying more on her instincts than her skill, she shouted, "Don't you manhandle me! I'll tell Cheng Lu! And then we'll see what happens!"

At the Hawaiian's name, the first man ceased to move except to take Ruggles's gun out of his holster and point it at him. "Get Peng to call Hawaii," he ordered the second man.

Sylvia, knowing that it would be only a matter of seconds before her association with Cheng Lu was revealed to be non-existent, shouted again as she stepped forward and began to turn sideways. "You tell him," she said, stepping forward and raising her right arm as if to point at him, "Sylvia says 'Hello' and tell him also that I said you are a bunch of bungling fools." The Beretta was ready to be fired, but she could not sight the gun that was still inside her purse. Nobody regarded a pointed purse as a threat of any kind, and Sylvia simply fired hitting one man in the upper arm, and then, jerking her trigger finger repeatedly, she fired wildly at the other man who ducked and waited for her to empty the clip. He moved towards her outstretched arm, grabbed it, and flung Sylvia against the wall which she slid down until she was sitting on the floor. Ruggles, already on the floor, stayed there, hyperventilating in rhythm to the bossa nova music.

The call to Hawaii was cancelled. "I told you to search this place!" Doctor Peng snarled as he entered the room. Sylvia recognized him immediately. "Fool," Peng said angrily at the man who had been shot in the shoulder. "You're bleeding all over the floor!" The other worker left to search the area. Peng called after him, "Bring some paper towels here...now!"

Peng waited until the man returned. He pressed the towels against the injured man's wound. "Well," he said to Sylvia, "the nosy amateur!" When the other man came back saying that there was no one else on the premises, he said, "Let's get these idiots into the back and then get this place cleaned up thoroughly. I want no trace of anything that went on in here." He picked up the bottle of Bollinger, the cake, and the utensils and put them into the basket. He pulled the iPod out of the speakers and pushed everything down into the picnic basket. "Leave nothing behind in here." He turned to the wounded man. "You... you get back there and I'll see how bad it is. Just don't bleed on anything!"

The uninjured man waited for an order. Peng pointed at Wilfred Ruggles. "Put this idiot on his feet or just drag him back. I'll take her. I want to know how they got in here."

Ruggles, convinced that this was some scare tactic that Sylvia's husband had arranged, babbled, "Nothin' happened! The gal came onto me!" Then he shouted at Sylvia, "Tell him! Your old man went to a lot of trouble for nothin'!"

The man grabbed Ruggles' arm, twisting it behind him as he pulled him to his feet. He jerked him and shouted, "Shut up!" as he began to march him toward the back room.

Joseph Peng had taken Sylvia by the hair and pulled her to her feet. Half dragged and half stumbling, she, too, was delivered to the back room and shoved into a chair.

Ruggles was tossed onto the floor. "Easy, fellas," Wilfred shouted, "I can explain!"

Peng kicked Ruggles. "How did she get in here?"

"I don't know what she was after," he yelled. "I kept it in my pants! Tell him I kept it in my pants!" he shouted at Sylvia. "She tempted me... but I didn't take the bait. *I kept it in my pants!*"

Sylvia Maitlin who had never uttered a four-letter word in her life, found herself to be so disgusted that only the pronunciation of a forbidden four-letter word could release the tension of revulsion. "Shut the fuck up!" she hissed at him.

Peng lost his temper. He turned to Sonya. "How did you get in here?"

Sylvia snapped at him. "How do you expect her to answer with a gag in her mouth?"

Peng slapped Sylvia hard across the face. "Then you tell me. How did you get in here and who is outside waiting for you?" He saw the Beretta peeking out from the hole it had blown in the side of her purse. He opened her purse and took out the gun. "How did you get in here?"

Sylvia clenched her teeth and would not respond.

He pointed the gun at Ruggles. "I will count to five and you'll tell me what I want to know or I'll shoot him. One... two... three--"

Sylvia knew there were no more bullets in the gun. "Go ahead! Shoot!" she shouted. "And you'll bring the cops in here quick. They expected the first shots. But we should have been outside by now. Go ahead! Shoot! You'll bring 'em right in."

Ruggles squealed, "You got the wrong man! I kept my pants on!"

"Four.... Five." He did not shoot. "For the last time…how did you get in?"

Sonya tried to say, "Tell him!" but it came out as only two garbled grunts. "Wuhh wuh!"

Joseph Peng ordered that her gag be removed. As soon as it was, Sonya gasped, "From the shed outside the old kitchen door! There's no need to hurt anyone. There's a sewer there!"

Peng picked up a flashlight and walked to the kitchen. He saw the door standing ajar. He went into the shed and saw the manhole cover lying beside an open hole. The flashlight illuminated the ladder and the sewer - neither of which he had known about. "Damn! There's a sewer here," he shouted. "Gao never told me about this sewer! I can hear the water! All right. Bring the old guy here! If there are cops out there we can get rid of these carcasses right now!"

Ruggles was dragged to the shed. "Toss him down the hole!" Peng shouted.

Ruggles, begging for help and forgiveness, was tossed headfirst down the hole into the sewer. A splash was heard. Peng and the man returned to the workroom.

Peng pointed at Sylvia. "She's next... and the fool whose brains you bashed in. Throw them both down the hole, too. And if our Chinese girlfriend won't talk, she'll be next."

The first man retrieved Sensei's unconscious body and picked him up, carrying him out through the kitchen. He tossed him down into the sewer, not realizing that Ruggles, upright in the water, was able to catch the falling man. Then he returned for Sylvia.

Again, marching her by the hair, she was forced through the kitchen and into the shed. She kicked violently as he tried to force her into the shed. Finally, he knocked her down, grabbed both her ankles, and held her up in the air; and as if he were driving a post hole-digger, plunged her down the hole. Sylvia landed in three feet of water - enough to cushion her fall. Dazed she stood up and grabbed one of the ladder's rungs.

Peng was still holding the Beretta and the flashlight as he came and stood over the opening. He illuminated the area around the base of the ladder; but Sylvia, seeing her dry suit lying across one of the ladder's supports, had already snatched it and, concealing herself behind the ladder, had begun to put it on. The wounded man came up behind him. "Where does this sewer lead?" Peng asked.

"Sewer is old... since before World War number Two. Water goes like waterfall over a cliff a mile down. Dead end."

Peng, not realizing that the Beretta was empty, thought that if he wanted to shoot her, he would have to descend into the sewer to do it. "Enjoy the rats," he said, and, thinking that he'd soon be opening it to toss Sonya down, decided to push the manhole cover only half way across the opening.

Nearly an hour had passed since they first went into the sewer. George took Terrell's Smith & Wesson and told him to wait in the van while he went down to the museum to see what was happening. "It's not loaded," Terrell confessed.

"What do you mean?" George asked incredulously. "Sylvia bought you a new box of rounds."

"Statistics show that you're more likely to get shot if you're carrying a weapon. And we've broken enough laws. I don't want to be arrested for murder."

"You are a bloody fool," George said. "Where are the bullets?"

"Back at the house. I'm not sorry. I probably saved lives!"

George took the gun anyway and as quickly as he could, jogged down the street. As he approached the museum he could see a figure emerge from the front staff entrance. The figure circled the building and, satisfied that there were no police cars waiting, went back into the building. In another minute he re-emerged carrying a stack of gift-wrapped boxes. He walked to the Toyota, put the boxes on the passenger's seat, and drove off.

George called Terrell and reported the activity. "I'm going in," he said. "Something is definitely wrong."

In the sewer, Sylvia was able to pull Sensei's unconscious body away from the totally confused Ruggles and to prop and wedge his body between the ladder and the wall. Ruggles waded to the far side of the sewer and tried to sit down. Since the manhole cover had only partially been placed over the aperture, there was an extremely dim light down in the sewer. Sylvia put on her night-vision goggles and made sure that Sensei's head was safely above water. She could hear the distant rumbling of water entering the sewer line and thought that there had probably been a cloudburst farther up the mountain. Knowing that the wave of water would strike them soon, she quickly finished putting on the dry suit and removed the goggles so that she could secure the suit's head covering. She replaced the goggles and in another moment they were engulfed by a high wave of rushing water. She had no way of knowing how long the flood would last. She did know that there was no way that she could release the unconscious man in order to help Ruggles who had been swept - she did not know how far - down the sewer line by the raging water. She held Sensei securely against the ladder and waited for the flood to subside.

When Sensei had entered the museum, he hung his goggles on his belt with a carabiner. The goggles had a wide headband that Sylvia hoped would give his head some protection. She unhitched them and began to secure them to his head. Again, she looked around for Ruggles, but could not see him. A second wave of water was rushing towards them. She braced herself and held Sensei tightly. As the wave passed, she heard Ruggles groan in the distance. She searched for him in the pale green light of her glasses, calling his name. In the confines of the channel, her voice took on an echo quality, but she continued to repeat Ruggles' name so that he could follow the sound of her voice in the darkness. Ruggles had been washed down the waterway a hundred feet before he was able to grab a tree root that had penetrated the sewer's wall. He faintly called out, "Help!"

Sylvia heard him and answered. "It's all right, Wilfred. I'm here." Her voice, in the tunnel's peculiar acoustics, had a soft and sultry quality. With her goggles on, she could barely see him in the distance. Ruggles groaned as he then began to crawl back to the museum's egress point. Sylvia called again with the same echoing weirdness, "I can see you, Wilfred. Keep on coming. Keep on coming. We're waiting for you."

George, walking with the casual lope of a man going to work, approached the staff's door, and, finding it locked, proceeded to ring the emergency bell. George waited on the side of the doorway to see who would answer the bell.

It was Joseph Peng who came to see who had rung the bell. "Chin?" he called, opening the door.

George stepped out of the darkness and jammed the Smith & Wesson into his side as he grabbed and turned him into a choke-hold with his strong left arm. Dragging Peng along, George whispered to his captive, "Holler back that you're gonna help change a tire."

"They're too far back," Peng heaved for breath. "They won't hear me."

"Then get out your phone and call the woman and tell her - in English - that you're gonna help Chin change a tire on his car and you'll be right back."

With George's arm still around his neck, Peng reached for his cellphone and touched Sylvia's Beretta in his pocket. George was still behind him. He'd have to wait to take a shot at him. He got out his cellphone and called the back room. "Chin's got a flat tire. I'm going to help him. I'll be right back." George could hear the response, "Ok."

As Peng returned the cell phone to his pocket, he grabbed the Beretta, twisted out of George's grip, and pointed the gun at George. George lowered his weapon. Peng chuckled. "You're an intruder." He squeezed the trigger and the Beretta clicked.

George laughed with relief. "My turn," he said as Peng sank to his knees and begged for his life. George hit him on the head with the gun. Then he clasped the back of Peng's collar and dragged him back towards the repair room.

As he neared the room he could hear a man and a woman speaking in Chinese. He moved closer to the sound. When Sensei and Sonya had approached the room, they had come from the side; but George was approaching it in a direct perpendicular line. He moved closer. The voices seemed to be arguing. Whenever there was a lull in the conversation, George did not move for fear of making a noise. As soon as the talking resumed, he continued to walk softly down the corridor to the repair and storage room. He dropped Peng onto the floor as he neared the entryway.

The room's wide doors were standing open. George entered and moved to the side, concealing himself behind some tapestries that hung from an overhead line. Immediately he encountered a chair that was positioned at a table on which lay a scale, an opened "brick" of a white powder, a glass-cutting surface and an assortment of baggies and tools. George could not see the complete table, but he realized that it was the workplace for preparing the distribution of what an ornate red Ming jar had contained. As he hid behind the Chinese tapestries, he could see Sonya across the room, some twenty feet from him. The wounded man, his upper arm tied with a white cloth tourniquet, held a semi-automatic weapon across his lap. The girl was leaning against the desk. She held a revolver - it had been Ruggles' gun - which she pointed at Sonya as she taunted her in Chinese.

A slit between two hanging "wall" tapestries allowed George to see without being seen. The wounded man and the girl were turned away from him, but Sonya was looking right in his direction. He flicked a finger and she widened her eyes. He could see that her hands and ankles were taped together and that there was a gag in her mouth. She saw his eyes staring at her and she began to blink her eyes.

Again George watched Sonya blink. She was definitely trying to tell him something. He detected a pattern. Three short blinks, followed by three long blinks, followed by three short blinks. She stared at him with a desperate expression on her face. 1,2,3 pause, 4… 5… 6…, pause, 7,8,9. "Jesus," he suddenly realized, "she's sending me a message in Morse Code. SOS." It wouldn't be the Boy Scout version. She'd use the International Morse Code, the one that he had reviewed in the Police Academy.

"Everybody knows S O S," he thought. "And yes… there's a trick to memorizing the Morse Code. But what the hell was it?" How was he supposed to remember a mnemonic? "You idiot," he chastised himself, "you're *supposed* to remember a mnemonic!" He repeated the S O S and could see Sonya express gratitude in her eyes. Then she long-blinked twice. "Dash, Dash," George told himself. What was two dashes? Mom Ma! M. Then she blinked dash dot dash dash. What did that mean? He shook his head from side to side. She tried again and this time she raised and lowered her head. Up and down. Dash dot dash dash. He got it. A yo yo. Yo Yip Yo Yo. Y. She evidently learned the same mnemonic as he had learned. M and Y equaled My.

My. She blinked dash, dash, dot. Going Going Git! G. He tried to reason the meaning from likely possibilities. Her what? Her gun? He remembered "U" and tried dot dot dash. Ya Ya You. Sonya nodded.

George swept away the scattering of recriminations he had wanted to hurl at Terrell for his stupidity at refusing to load the S&W. All this half-assed liberal baloney! But he had no time to bitch about guns. Sonya was blinking again… a long blink. That would be Trail for T. Then a dot followed by a dash. Clearly Ah Ahh. A. That was enough for George. My Gun Ta… had to be "My gun is on the table." He moved laterally so that he could see the far end of the table. And there, in full view, was Sonya's fanny pack. He stepped back to where she could see him and nodded. Immediately, Sonya began to writhe and grunt and otherwise distract her captors. No one saw George reach out and grab the fanny pack, bring it back into the shadows, open it, and remove the Colt.

Sonya continued to gag violently and writhe as if in pain. The man told the girl to loosen her gag so that she could tell them what was wrong. The woman put the revolver into her belt and began to untie Sonya's gag. Still there was no way that George could step into the room without putting Sonya at risk. The wounded man's left arm was bandaged and George could see the way he held the weapon, he was obviously right handed.

The gag was loosened and the girl pulled the revolver from her belt and pointed it into Sonya's face. The tone of her voice indicated that she wanted Sonya to tell her what she was making such a commotion about. The wounded man laid his weapon in his lap to tend to the bandage that circled his upper arm. This was George's only opportunity. He stepped into the room and acting as if he were not alone, he shouted, "Get 'em from the other side!" The girl stood up, pointed the revolver at him, and looked to the side. As she looked back, he fired the Colt and she crumbled to the floor. The other man put his hands up. "Easy, DEA! I'm an agent with the DEA. I don't have credentials on me. I know who she is. She's Sonya Lee, an agent from Hong Kong."

"You asshole," George said, angry that he had come so close to killing a law enforcement agent. "Untie her!" He checked to see if the girl he had shot was dead. Straight on, the bullet had entered her forehead.

"I can't untie her," the agent whispered. "You've got to make it look like you're arresting me."

George looked at his oriental features and his proximity to the girl. "Are you the guy who invaded the Maitlins' house... you and your dead girlfriend?"

"Yeah. I wanted to be sure they weren't hurt. I used old zip ties that they could have gotten out of."

"Did you kill that dog?"

"I had to."

"Then let me put the cuffs on you and make this look right." George tossed the agent down on the floor and not too gently forced his wrists into one of the zip ties that Sonya had in her fanny pack.

Sonya kept trying to spit the remainder of the gag from her mouth. Finally George untied the gag and she yelled, "Undo my restraints! Sylvia's in the sewer along with Percy and the guard. Percy's hurt bad."

George took off his belt and inserted the buckle's prong along the zip tie's ridges until it dislodged the locking mechanism from the slot it had wedged into. As soon as Sonya's hands were free, she tore the tape off her ankles. The tape had cut off the circulation in her legs and she had to wait until it was restored before she could walk. "You stay here and guard these two" George ordered as he took out his phone and called 9-1-1 as he walked to the kitchen to find the entrance to the sewer. Sonya was not happy having to stay with Peng and the DEA agent. She picked up the revolver the girl had used and leaned against the desk.

In the nearly pitch black sewer, Sylvia had been guiding Wilfred Ruggles forward with a soft coaxing echo. "I'll tell you when the next flood will come. Don't worry. Just keep coming towards me. Follow my voice." Wilfred gingerly crept forward in the water, being led by the Siren-nymph quality of her voice.

Suddenly George flicked on the kitchen light and immediately enough light entered the sewer for Wilfred Ruggles to see what Sylvia's voice had emanated from. In her latex head covering and other worldly night vision goggles it was as though she had morphed into an alien being. He gasped in terror at the sight of her and at Sensei, too, who also seemed to be penetrating him with Xray vision or something similar. He was still making the squeals and shudders of terror when George pulled the cover completely off the hole and called down, "Sylvia! Perce!"

"We're here," Sylvia said, pulling off the goggles. "But Sensei is unconscious. Call an ambulance!"

Terrell Maitlin's van drove up to the door just after the first police cruiser arrived. Maitlin bolted from his car and ran to the door. "It's the Commissioner," one officer shouted and followed him.

Maitlin ran to the kitchen. "George!" he shouted.

"We're out in the shed. Help me to get Sensei up. He's wounded."

The officer climbed down the ladder and lifted Sensei up high enough for Terrell and George to pull him onto the floor. The officer then helped Sylvia up the ladder. He looked at Ruggles. "Is this guy dead?" Ruggles made a croaking sound and the officer helped him to get up the ladder.

Police cars had surrounded the museum. Sonya's eye needed medical attention and she was taken into the ambulance with Sensei. "Percy," she kept repeating.

A second ambulance took Wilfred Ruggles and the undercover "prisoner" to the hospital. George told no one that the prisoner was in fact a DEA agent, and he was treated and booked.

A yellow crime scene tape circled the museum as the girl's body was removed and Doctor Peng was taken into custody. The forensic team would likely not be finished its work at the site until the following day. George told Terrell Maitlin who pointedly told the police chief to intercept the drug courier before he crossed into Canada. He gave him the Toyota's model and license number and, repeating the intel given to George by the wounded agent, indicated the complicity of Doctor Gao and Orville Banning and Harriet Yong who owned the Toyota. Terrell Maitlin had the additional "honor" of informing the DEA that their agent was now being held in the county jail.

Sylvia wanted her husband to wait in the bedroom while she showered. She insisted that she would "absolutely fall apart" if he left her side. Terrell Maitlin sat on his wife's side of the bed and listened to her sing in the shower, something she had never done before. Something wasn't adding up. Sylvia, while pretending to be "a shrinking violet" was acting more like one of those carnivorous plants. Terrell Maitlin had the uneasy feeling that he no longer was required to protect her but was, if he let his guard down, someone from whom he might actually need protection.

Perhaps, he thought, he could take up archery. Maybe some karate, too.

George went to the hospital to be with Sensei and Sonya. Sensei had sustained a severe concussion and although X-rays and MRI's revealed that his skull had not been fractured and that there was no intra-cranial bleeding, he still had not regained consciousness and would be kept in the hospital for observation. The three-inch laceration in his scalp was sutured.

Sonya's eye was examined and treated by a specialist. She asked the nurses if they would mind if she showered in their dressing room and they agreed, giving her fresh scrubs to wear. They saw all of her credentials and, when she begged to be allowed to stay in the ICU, they obliged. She then lay beside Sensei on the bed.

"Get some sleep," the nurse said. "If he's conscious by morning he'll probably be moved to a private room."

George had finished answering questions and came to the ICU to sit in a chair at the side of the room and wait for news about Sensei's prognosis.

SATURDAY, SEPTEMBER 17, 2011

It was after midnight when a DEA agent came to Sensei's room to awaken Sonya who was still sleeping beside him. The nurses had objected to her being disturbed, explaining that she, too, had been the victim of macing. "Her eyes are only now recovering," the ICU nurse advised.

George had sat at the side of the room in a chair, gently snoozing. He spoke softly to the agent. "Now is not the time to disturb them. Your own agent can fill you in."

The DEA agent refused to leave. "I'll handle this," the agent said gruffly to George. "Go back to sleep."

"Ain't nobody gonna be sleeping if you disturb him while she's around," George warned.

The agent looked contemptuously at George. "She's not a U.S. citizen. She doesn't have diplomatic immunity; and you ought to mind your own business." He bent over Sonya and said, "Wake up!"

The head nurse put her hand on his shoulder. "Get out of here or I'll call Security and have you arrested. Get out now!"

The agent was not intimidated. "And I'll have you arrested for interfering with an agent in the performance of his duty. Get the hell away from me!"

Sonya woke up. "What's going on?" She looked around and took a moment to appraise the situation. "What do you want?" she asked.

The agent reached across her and tugged at Sensei's arm. "You awake, buddy?"

"Don't you touch him," Sonya threatened.

"Look," he said, "Nothing's wrong with you. You can come out here and answer a few questions or I can call some U.S. Marshals to come in here and drag you out. You're a foreign agent and this is U.S. soil. I'm ordering you to get out of that bed now."

Sonya ignored him. She felt Sensei stirring.

The agent raised his voice. "I'm telling you to get out of that bed!"

"My name is Sonya Lee. Have you heard of me?"

"Yes. You're a Custom's agent."

"Is that all you know about me?"

"Yes. Cut the crap. Come out here now and answer a few questions."

Instantaneously, Sonya's leg shot out, her foot kicking him in the groin. He had not expected the attack and skidded backwards, doubled over. Now she was on her feet, flying towards him to kick him again squarely on the shoulder, sending him out the door, sprawling finally on the corridor floor. "I'll speak to you after he speaks to me!"

She came back to bed as the nurse shut the door.

"At's my girl," Sensei whispered.

Sonya Lee burst out crying. "Percy!" she wailed. "Oh, Percy! You've come back to me!"

George got up and left the ICU. He helped the agent to regroup himself and stand. Putting his hand on the man's arm, he said, "Let's go down to the cafeteria for some coffee. You don't want this story to get around, and you have no idea how sickening it can get when the two of them are conscious at the same time. By the way, have you been apprised of the involvement of Cheng Lu of Honolulu? He may be the mastermind behind this scheme. Let's just go down for coffee and I'll fill you in as best I can."

Terrell Maitlin did not know whether or not he appreciated his wife's new persona. Increasingly, she affected a frontiersman's manner of speaking. In a television interview, she began by being magnanimous in victory, a generosity she did not extend to certain media scandal-mongers who, she said, were less interested in truth than they were in "ass-kissing pseudo-experts." She began to lapse into a quasi-western gun moll manner of speaking. "I coulda' done more," she allowed, "but I only winged one of 'em. And ain't it a shame that there was no lawman on the job to do the shootin'." She did not disclose that it was a federal agent she had "winged."

Terrell Maitlin braced for her to say something else that he would never live down. He winced when she ended her televised interview with the sage advice, "When ya knows ye'r right, ya knows ye'r right. I happen to know authentic Imperial Qing porcelain when I see it! And you can take that to the bank. Lock and load, fellas. Thank you very much."

Sonya Lee stayed in Sensei's room. A man from the Chinese consulate came. She spoke to him in an imperial manner and he abruptly left. Later, the DEA agent gingerly approached her again and this time she answered all his questions. She also answered the questions of a gentleman from the State Department.

SUNDAY, SEPTEMBER 18, 2011

As Sensei lay, fully conscious in bed in the Maitlins' guest room, everyone gathered around him. "How did the jar get sold to Ezra Zhen?" he asked.

Terrell answered. "It was Dr. Gao's error. Apparently he doesn't know as much about Chinese porcelain as he thought he did. Peng uncrated the jar, dissolved the gel and removed the packs of heroin and left the jar on a table. So the jar was sitting there away from the big plastic bag that contained the liquified gel and the styrofoam square and crate. Peng was concerned with getting the heroin processed and left the cleaning up to Gao. But when Gao was selecting jars to be auctioned off to the dealers, he looked inside the Qing jar and, seeing that it was empty and never imagining that Peng was so slovenly as to leave the genuine jar on a table unattended, he told his workers - one of whom was a DEA agent - to re-crate it; and the workers obliged. It was sold to Ezra Zhen who evidently has a crush on my wife. He knew she wanted the jar and as long as she'd give him what he paid for it, he went ahead and did her the favor - never knowing what a hornet's nest would be stirred up. End of story."

Sylvia held her husband's hand. "I've talked to the museum in Philadelphia. I told them that everybody here wants to see the famous jar... so I'm letting our museum display it here for six months; but if they want to come and get it after that, they can have it." She turned to Sonya, "How much longer will you be with us? There's so much I'd like to show you. Seattle is such a wonderful place."

"I'm going back tomorrow," Sonya said. "My government is anxious to question me. For once nobody from Hong Kong was involved. They're still chapped about that slimy Dr. Peng and the way he tried to divert

108

attention from the fake jar by comparing my country to a third-world country like Nigeria. That did not go over well in Beijing."

George sat on a chair with a tablet. "So, Agent Lee, remind me again what the trick is for memorizing Morse Code."

"The mnemonics just apply so strangely. You don't ever forget them."

They laughed and recited the memory trick they had learned.

A   ah ahhhh. . – dot dash

B   boom bang bang bang – . . . dash dot dot dot

C   coo chi coo chi – . – . dash dot dash dot

D   dog doo doo – . . dash dot dot

E   eyeball . dot

F   fee fi foooo fum . . – . dot dot dash dot

G   going going git! – – . dash dash dot

H   ha, ha, ha, ha . . . . dot dot dot dot

I   snake-eyes . . dot dot

J   Ju Julie Julie Julie . – – – dot dash dash dash

K   kand ee kane – . – dash dot dash

L   la loo la la . – . . dot dash dot dot

M   mom mah – – dash dash

N   nein no – . dash dot

O   Oh, Oh, Oh – – – dash dash dash

P   pee poopoo pee . – – . dot dash dash dot

Q   quack quack quaaah quack . . – . dot dot dash dot

R   rev-ER-ie . – . dot dash dot

S   stac-ca-to . . . dot dot dot

T   Trail – dash

U   ya, ya. you . . – dot dot dash

V   Victory and Beethoven's Vth . . . – dot dot dot dash

W   we want work . – – dot dash dash

X   EX pan ded IT – . . – dash dot dot dash

Y   yo yip yo yo – . – – dash dot dash dash

Z   ze-braz eyez – – . . dash dash dot dot